GRAVE CREATURES

AN IAN DEX SUPERNATURAL THRILLER BOOK 2

JOHN P. LOGSDON

CHRISTOPHER P. YOUNG

CRIMSON MYTH
PRESS

Published by: Crimson Myth Press (www.CrimsonMyth.com)

Cover art: Jake Logsdon (www.JakeLogsdon.com)

Thanks to the Ian Dex Crew!
(listed in alphabetical order by first name)

Cassandra Hall
Hal Bass
John Debnam
Marie McCraney
Mike Helas
Natalie Fallon
Noah Sturdevant
Paulette Kilgore
Soobee Dewson

Thanks to the *Grave Creatures* Reader Team!
(listed in alphabetical order by first name)

Adam Goldstein, Adam Saunders-Pederick, Allen Stark, Amy Robertson, Andrew Greeson, Bob Topping, Bonnie Dale Keck, Brandy Dalton, Carmen Romano, Caroline Watson, Carolyn Fielding, Carolyn Jean Evans, Debbie Tily, Del Mitchell, Denise King, Hal Bass, Helen Day, Ian Nick Tarry, Jacky Oxley, Jamie Gray, Jodie Stackowiak, John Debnam, Kate Smith, Kathryne Nield, Kevin Frost, Marie McCraney, Mark Beech, Mark Brown, Martha Hayes, MaryAnn Sims, Megan McBrien, Mike Helas, Natalie Fallon, Noah Sturdevant, Paula Pruitt Jackson, Paulette Kilgore, Penny Campbell-Myhill, Ruth Nield, Sandee Lloyd, Sara Pateman, Scott Ackermann, Scott Reid, Stephen Bagwell, Wendy Schindler.

CHAPTER 1

*O*ne of the things I despised most about being on the Las Vegas Paranormal Police Department, better known as the PPD, was having to see the psychiatrist. Supposedly this was necessary in order to help us avoid losing our minds with all of the stuff that we see walking the beat, but most of us were inherently nuts anyway, which is why we made a perfect fit for the force.

But like any good cop, I took my place on the couch and let Dr. Vernon sift through my naughty thoughts. It was mandatory after any big cases anyway, and since it started a few hours after nightfall, I managed to be okay with it. If anything, I imagined that Dr. Vernon disliked having to stay late in order to take care of the PPD officers.

"For clarification," she said in her bookish way, "the mage that you faced was more powerful than any you've encountered in the past?"

"By far," I answered as the memory of Reese and his team of demons, or as I'd dubbed them "Admiral Psycho and The Four Demon Batteries," were hard to forget. "The guy was supremely confident, up until the end anyway."

"And this has led you to feel a sense of inferiority?"

"No," I said, bolting upright and giving her a look that suggested maybe she should be the one in therapy. "Where'd you get that idea?"

Dr. Vernon peered over her book.

The amethyst eyes that sat nestled in her deep brown cheeks were mesmerizing. They played off perfectly with her studious outfits, today's being a white button up shirt under a dark gray jacket that had a matching skirt. It was all rather form fitting, and she had quite a form. Unfortunately, she didn't get involved with patients.

She flipped back a few pages and said, "You noted that you believed there was no way for your team to defeat him. Then you said that you feared that you, specifically, felt incapable of protecting members of your crew. And just a minute ago you expressed frustration over the fact that you couldn't spend more time dealing with one of the mage's minions."

"So?"

"So why would you need to spend more time with one of the minions unless you felt some need to connect?" She had an eyebrow raised. I was about to reply, but she held up a finger. "Mr. Dex, when a person threatens our very existence, it's normal to want to identify with them. We seek to find a connection. Our psyche must deal with the fact that we're about to end. We need meaning." She paused, closing her book and leaning forward. "Do you understand what I mean?"

"Sure I do," I said, having been in that very situation more than once, "but that's not the case this time."

"I've heard that response many times over my years in practice, Mr. Dex."

"Not from me, you haven't," I replied, lying back down on the comfy leather couch.

"Okay," she said with a sigh. "Explain to me why you believe you desired to spend time with this minion."

I smiled to myself at the memory. "Because she was a seven-foot tall succubus with a body to die for…literally."

She frowned and then groaned. "So you're telling me this is some sort of sexual thing for you?"

"Well, duh, doc," I replied with a laugh. "I've been coming to these sessions with you for, what, seven years? You know my genetic alterations not only make me the most unique supernatural in the world, it also makes me a major horndog."

When joining the PPD, each officer is given genetic enhancements to accentuate their particular skills. Mages become more powerful, werewolves get added strength, vampires gain speed, and so on. We all improve, but there is a cost. Our libidos shoot up. I know it sounds odd, but it's true. For each element of your genome that gets enhanced, you get a power point added to your sexual desire. So if you get bumped up in strength and stamina, you get two horny points along with that. Now, that may not seem like much, but it is, and I got it the worst…or best, depending on your perspective. I'm an amalgamite, meaning I have tons of genetic upgrades since I'm a jack of all trades. I have speed, power, night vision, special skills, the ability to do minor magic, and I'm a snappy dresser. Okay, that last one isn't exactly a factor of my genome, but it needed to be said. Anyway, the point is that I've got a plus-10 on the horniness scale (well, technically it's a plus-11, but who's counting?). This is tough because a lot of the people who work for me are incredibly gorgeous and highly desirable. Unfortunately, I'm the boss, meaning they reside in the no-touch zone. They all play amongst themselves as they see fit, seeing that they're peers, but being that I'm the chief…. Well, I can't go down that road.

Dr. Vernon leaned back again and put on a wry grin.

"What?" I said, suddenly feeling like I was about to lose an argument.

"The minion was a succubus," she answered while writing something in her book.

"Yeah, so?"

"So what does a succubus do, Mr. Dex?"

"Do you really want me to go there, Doc?"

"A succubus controls the one she is manipulating," Dr. Vernon explained as if I didn't know this already. "Therefore, I was correct in my assessment."

I furrowed my brow. "Huh?"

"You were feeling a sense of inferiority!"

Technically that was true, but it wasn't for the reasons she was originally claiming.

I rolled my eyes at her and faced the ceiling again.

It wasn't easy being me, but it was fun. I had the best job in the world, along with a fantastic crew. Yes, I had an annoying psychoanalyst and my bosses, the Directors, could be trying at times, but they were all just a wrinkle in an otherwise dream situation.

"Babycakes," came the voice of Lydia through the internal communications channel, "are you there?"

Lydia was a culmination of the best artificial intelligence available, 100% digital, a miracle of technology, and the only non flesh and bone member of the squad. She spoke to me through a device implanted in my brain called a "connector." All PPD agents had them. They allowed us to communicate with each other over long distances without the need to carry additional gadgetry. Though Lydia was A.I., she often flirted with me. Specifically me. Everyone else on the force got the standard robotic drone whenever they spoke with her.

"…and this is why you still have issues, Mr. Dex," continued Dr. Vernon.

"One sec, Doc," I said. "Getting a call from base. What's going on Lydia?"

"We've received a report that there are a group of corpses digging themselves out of their graves in old town."

"What?"

"You heard me right, sugar," Lydia replied sweetly. "Dead people are coming up in one of the cemeteries."

"You're talking about zombies, right?"

"You know it, puddin'."

"Well, that doesn't sound good," I said as I stood up and looked at Dr. Vernon. "Sorry, Doc, I gotta run."

"You do realize there is no such thing as zombies, Mr. Dex?" she said.

"Seems there are. My top-of-the-line A.I. doesn't make mistakes. She's the icing on the cake, the best of the best, and all that."

"Aw," said Lydia in response, "you're so sweet, lover."

"But Mr. Dex," Dr. Vernon exclaimed, "we haven't dealt with your issues yet!"

I laughed as I stopped at the door. "Doc, you of all people know that I've got more issues than you'll ever clear up in a lifetime."

And with that, I rushed out of the building.

CHAPTER 2

*T*took the stairs two at a time as I rushed down to the main floor. I had to get out of there before Dr. Vernon came after me. It wasn't likely that she would, but why chance it? It was a certainty that she'd note on my record that we hadn't finished our session. The Directors would give me crap about that, no doubt.

"Lydia," I said as I pushed out the main door, "you're a genius."

"I know, darlin'."

"No, I mean you're seriously a genius." I flipped open the door to my red Aston Martin Rapide S and climbed inside. The engine purred to life, reminding me why I'd purchased it in the first place. "Helping me get out of there by using a zombie reference? Classic!"

"Sweetie," she said in a calmer voice, "I wasn't making that up. There actually *are* reports of people digging themselves out of their graves."

I laughed at that as I pulled out of my parking spot. "Great stuff."

Anyone who knew me was aware that I loved a good gag. Pulling one over on Dr. Vernon was great. I couldn't help but picture the good doctor sitting in her high-backed, leather chair right now while frowning at the door and wondering what the heck had just happened. Knowing her, she'd just write yet another note in my file about how I was unfit to be a public servant. Unfortunately for her, nobody on my crew was fit to be a public servant, which is precisely what made us so damn good at our jobs.

"Ian, you there?" It was the voice of my partner, Rachel Cress.

"Hey, Rachel, did you hear the gem that Lydia came up with to get me out of the psych eval? It was brilliant." I cackled again. "She said that there are zombies climbing out of their graves. Zombies!"

"There are," Rachel replied, deadpan, causing me to laugh again. "Ian, Lydia wasn't making that up. It's actually happening."

At this point it was all I could do to maintain my composure.

Zombies.

Hilarious.

My guess was that they were both playing off the fact that I loved zombie movies. All kinds, too. The old ones, the new ones, the silly ones…it didn't matter. They were all fun to me.

"We're not joking, Ian," Rachel said tightly.

"We really aren't, honey bubbles," agreed Lydia.

"Honey bubbles?" Rachel had said it in a disgusted tone of voice. "What the hell does that even mean?"

Lydia's voice returned to being pedantic. "They are bubbles made of honey, Ms. Cress."

"Ugh."

A little voice in my head noted something odd, which I wouldn't have noticed if Lydia hadn't called me "honey bubbles" and Rachel hadn't grumbled about it.

In order for the zombie thing to be a joke, Rachel and Lydia would have needed to be colluding. That was fishy because Rachel and Lydia didn't get along.

On top of that, Lydia had never lied to me before.

Maybe there'd been an upgrade to her software? That would be good, actually. It'd be fantastic to work with a flirty A.I. who also had a great sense of humor. Plus, if she'd learned to work more cordially with the rest of my team, that'd be a win. Not that it was her fault, of course. My crew, especially Rachel, tended to treat Lydia like she was nothing but a machine. While technically that was true, she *did* have a personality, and now and then she expressed emotion in such a way as to make her seem almost human.

So a software upgrade had to be it.

There must have been complaints put in about our friendly neighborhood A.I., most of them likely coming from Rachel. Fortunately, they hadn't removed her ability to flirt with me. I kind of liked that, especially since I had a self-imposed restriction from flirting with anyone else on the force.

"Ian?" pressed Rachel.

"Hmmm?" I said, jolting back out of my thoughts. "Oh, yeah, right. We've got zombies on our hands." Classic prank, but I'd play along. "Where should I meet you to see these creatures of the grave, Rachel?"

"King David Cemetery," she replied without inflection. "I've got the rest of the crew on the way."

"Oh, most definitely." I rolled my eyes. "We'll need everyone on this case."

I cruised down East Sunset to South Eastern, making my

way over to the cemetery. There was no point in rushing, so I took my time and let the wind blow through my hair.

If nothing else, it was a nice night for a zombie invasion. Of course it was almost always nice in Las Vegas, at least during the evenings, which happened to be when the Paranormal Police Department was primarily on duty.

I spotted the Don Tortaco Mexican Grill on my right and my stomach grumbled. A burrito sounded good right about now. I'd have to make a stop there on my way back from this practical joke my team was playing on me.

I grinned again.

Zombies was usually a joke played on new recruits, according to the notes I read from the previous chief of the PPD. It was done to make a person feel like they were part of the team. Apparently, though, a few recruits got pretty pissed off about it and so the previous chief had stopped the practice. This had all happened before I was born, though, so my team probably didn't know I was aware of all this.

From my perspective, the thought of them setting me up like this was sweet. It wasn't even my birthday or anything. Maybe it was boss-appreciation week? Is there even such a thing?

"The rest of the team is here, Ian," Rachel said. "Just waiting on you."

"I'm sure you are," I replied, shaking my head. "I'm about a minute away."

Taking a left on Eldorado Lane, I noticed a few people walking around in the graveyard. That was kind of odd, being that it was late at night, but some people worked days so visitation was done when it could be done. Of course, they could also have been actors.

Yeah, actors!

My crew was really laying this joke on thick.

I chuckled.

Finally, I turned right into the King David Cemetery, stopped my car, got out, brushed down my suit, and checked my shoes.

Then I walked up to the rest of the gang.

And that's when my blood froze.

CHAPTER 3

This was either the most extravagant practical joke ever played, or there really were zombies clomping around. My brain was having trouble accepting this, though, as it simply wasn't possible. People died and that was that. They didn't come back up out of the ground. That stuff just happened in the movies.

"Okay," I said, feeling that I knew the impending answer to the question I was about to pose, "if this isn't a prank, maybe it's a flashmob thing?"

Rachel frowned at me while keeping her arms crossed. "In the middle of the night at a graveyard this far off the strip?"

"They could be practicing."

I looked from face to face, seeing the same expression on each of them.

Rachel, Jasmine, and Felicia were leaning back against Felicia's blue '68 Camaro SS, looking like a Charlie's Angels poster. That brought back memories that were ill-fitting with being in a cemetery. Rachel was a mage with blond hair and sapphire eyes; Jasmine was also a mage, but she had black hair and emerald eyes, and her skin was starkly ivory; and Felicia's flawless dark-skin housed deep brown eyes that glowed red when she moved from her normal state into her werewolf one.

On the other side of me were Chuck and Griff, partners in the force and in life. How long they'd been dating, I didn't know, but I'd found out about it during a recent visit to the supernatural morgue when we were trying to stop demons from taking over the place.

Griff wore leathers like Rachel and Jasmine—it was a thing with mages—but his were more refined and less revealing. He was a clean cut guy who you'd never mistake as being a magic user. He was just too prim and proper. If anything, he looked like he belonged on a yacht in some Caribbean island while being served caviar by his butler.

Chuck was a tall vampire who wore a black overcoat and a wide-brimmed hat. It was almost as if the costume crew for *Indiana Jones* and *The Matrix* had gotten together and set up an ensemble for Chuck. He also had a bit of a goatee going on, which I had to admit looked kind of cool whenever his fangs came out.

"Maybe there's a movie being filmed?" I asked, but then looked around and answered my own question. "Nope, no cameras."

"I know this sounds dumb," said Chuck, "but is there such a thing as an apocalypse training exercise?"

The look that Griff gave him made me think they'd be having words later. "Even if there were such a thing, Charles, would those participating in such an event elect to be reanimated corpses?"

"Someone has to play that part, right?" Chuck countered.

"I have no response to that," said Griff slowly.

I pulled out Boomy, my 50-caliber Desert Eagle, checked the magazine, and pointed it at the head of the nearest supposed-zombie. I still wasn't 100% certain that my team was being on the up and up about this, but there was one way to find out.

"Right, then," I said, knowing they'd put an end to things before I fired my weapon at some poor actor, "may as well just blow this guy away, right?"

"Do you think that'll work?" asked Felicia.

"And should we do it anyway?" said Chuck. "It's not like these guys are hurting anyone. They're just walking around."

So they *were* playing me. I grinned.

"True, but you know how it is with zombies, eventually they'll start getting angry. It's what they do."

Jasmine turned to look at me. "Seriously?"

"Sure," I replied as I cracked my neck from side to side, pretending to be preparing to fire. "Don't you ever watch any movies on the subject?"

"I've seen quite a few," she answered. "I've also read numerous books on them, mostly fiction."

It was my turn to look at her. "You mean there are nonfiction books about them?"

Just then one of the creatures made a gurgling sound. It was pretty convincing. Whoever my team had gotten to play these roles were good. Real good. The choppy walking, the crazy outfits, the partially dug up graves, the smell, the sounds…. It was all top-notch.

Then, in unison, every one of the zombies froze.

My eye twitched. "Uh…what just happened?"

"I don't know, Ian," said Rachel, "but I have a bad feeling about this."

Enough was enough. I could take a joke just as well as anyone, but this was starting to lose its funny. Unless, of course, all the zombies were all about to dance to a rendition of *Thriller*. That would have been the cherry on top, for sure.

I waited.

No music.

I waited some more.

Still no music.

"Okay, guys," I said finally, staring to weary of this charade. "Tell me this is an elaborate joke and let's get on with it. You got me. Ha ha. Well-played. I've been bested. Etcetera, etcetera."

"No joke," said Chuck.

"Come on." The hairs on the back of my neck were sticking straight out. "Quit messing around. This has gone far enough."

"Ian," Griff whispered, "we are as perplexed about this as you are. There is no tomfoolery afoot."

I gulped and glanced around at the bodies standing like statues in the cemetery. There were about twenty of them, at least that I could see from here. The place wasn't exactly tiny, after all.

As an amalgamite, I had the ability to see quite well in dark situations, and I could lightly zoom my vision, too. Not like a pair of binoculars or anything, but much better than merely squinting.

I focused in on the nearest "zombie" and saw no animation at all. No breathing. No movement. Nothing. It was as still as stone. I zoomed in on the next one, and the next. None of them were moving. Not even slightly. They were literally dead still.

"Oh shit," I said after a hard swallow, "those things are fucking real!"

As if validating my statement, the entire collection of reanimated corpses turned toward us.

CHAPTER 4

The air was still and my senses were on overdrive. I was so jacked up that I could hear a gnat fart from a mile away.

"Something tells me the shit is about to hit the fan," Felicia said while slowly pulling out her Eagle.

"I can't believe this is happening," I said as my mouth ran dry. "Zombies aren't supposed to exist."

"Neither are werewolves, vampires, fae, mages…" Rachel said as her hands began to glow. "Shall I go on?"

My brain was struggling with this. We were standing in the middle of a graveyard off the beaten path of downtown Vegas staring down a mass of dead people who were all focused intently on us. This was no joke, no flashmob, no movie set, and more than likely not an apocalyptic preparation rally.

"Okay, okay," I said. "Jasmine, head?"

"What? Here?"

"I don't mean *that*," I hissed. And I'm supposed to be the dirty one? "You've watched the movies and read the books.

So have I. Do you agree that we should shoot them in the head?"

The zombie closest to us screeched something fierce, causing me to nearly crap my pants. Without thought, I pulled the trigger and let a breaker blow the damn thing's head in two.

It collapsed to the ground, unmoving.

"Yep," Jasmine said with a nod. "Definitely aim for the head."

We formed a semi-circle and began firing like mad as the things ran at us. The mages were laying down energy pulses and casting flaming pain wherever possible. They were just trying to slow the dead down long enough for the rest of us to blow their heads off. It worked on most of the creatures, but a few were getting through.

Chuck, Felicia, and I dropped down so we were under the stream of magical mayhem. There was no sense in getting caught in the crossfire, after all. We kept our breaker bullets streaming at them like there was no tomorrow. Of course, if this *was* an actual zombie apocalypse, maybe there would be no tomorrow. I shuddered at the thought.

My original guesstimate of twenty was clearly way off since the damn things kept coming. If they were digging out of the entire graveyard, we were going to lose this war. And I could only hope that this was the *only* graveyard affected right now.

"Griff," I called out, "can you cast a light over the area?"

He did.

Just as I expected, bodies were actively pushing up out of the dirt.

Griff moved the light around and we saw that not all of the graves were opening. The people I had seen when I'd turned on to Eldorado must have actually been visitors. Hopefully they weren't seeing what was happening here, or if they were, they had enough sense to get the hell out of the cemetery.

"I'm assuming you see…"

"I do," answered Griff. "Charles, I'll need you to cover me as I seek the source of this reckoning."

"Cover you?" I said after tagging a zombie through the neck with enough of an upward angle to blow out the back of his head. "Where the hell are you going?"

Griff continued scanning the grounds. "If I can locate the base of the power, I can shut it off. Much like one would do with a faucet."

"Or an overflowing toilet?" suggested Chuck.

"I'd prefer my less vulgar description, but that's the right of it."

Seeing that most of the dead were coming at us from a single angle, I saw no point in sending out two of my officers alone. We were all better off working together than splitting apart.

"We move as a team," I stated. Then I nodded at Griff. "You direct us, but we all move as one."

We crept along, keeping careful to unleash bullets at anything that came close. I couldn't imagine any non-dead individuals would be dumb enough to run toward us at this point, especially at night in a graveyard.

"Look out!" shouted Rachel as one of the creatures reached for Jasmine out of the shadows.

I jumped forward and dropkicked it so hard that my shoe came off, sticking in its chest cavity. It wasn't easy keeping your shoes nice in this line of work.

Felicia stepped over and dropped a bullet in the thing's skull.

She then reached down and pulled my shoe out of its chest and went to hand it to me.

"Uh, no thanks," I said, wincing. "I have another pair in the car."

"Why do you have an extra pair of shoes in the car?" Felicia asked, dropping the shoe.

"Because I like having options."

Again, she said, "Why?"

"Here," Griff interrupted. I looked over to see him kneeling while pointing at a very dim multicolored light that was running along the ground. "It's slowly moving across the cemetery. As it crosses over a grave, it reanimates the life inside."

"That's creepy," noted Chuck.

We were all nodding in agreement, mesmerized by the light until we realized that another batch of the bastards were on us.

"Fire!"

Heads were blown apart as the carnage piled up until Griff successfully tempered the source of the disturbance. Once the rainbowesque light ceased, so did the deceased...in a manner of speaking. At least the ones who had not fully made it out of their graves. Those just sank back into the dirt from where they were coming.

The ones above ground were eradicated within a couple of minutes.

That's when the world silenced again.

We all took a collective breath while trying to come to terms with what we'd just seen. I was even considering heading back to Dr. Vernon's office to unburden my thoughts about this one. She'd never believe it.

"What just happened?" I said, not expecting an answer.

Griff provided one anyway.

"Necromancy," he said as Chuck helped him to a nearby tombstone. He looked beat. "I've not seen this in a very long time."

"You say that like you're two hundred years old," I said, and then remembered that his personnel file marked him as closer to three hundred. "Never mind. Anyway, you were saying?"

"It's an old art. One of darkness. Communion with the dead." He paused as he glanced around. Finally, he whispered, "Unholy."

"Scary as hell, if you ask me." I was trying to be careful where I stepped, considering that I had only one shoe on. "These things aren't supposed to exist." I held up a warning hand at Rachel. "I know, I know. But still, *some* supernatural bullshit is just that: bullshit. Zombies? Come on. It was so ridiculous that when you first called me I thought for certain you guys were pulling a prank on me."

"Why would we do that?" Rachel asked.

"Hmmm?"

"Why would we be playing a trick on you?"

I began moving my shoeless foot around on a soft patch of grass.

"Good natured fun maybe?" I replied with a shrug. "Could have been boss-appreciation day or something."

They all gave me a you're-joking-right? look.

"Some employees do it," I said sullenly. "Anyway, my point is that nobody's going to believe this."

"On the contrary," Lydia said through the connector. "The Directors have heard what's happened and they're very interested in speaking with you."

I dropped my head forward and sighed.

"Lydia," I said as sweetly as I could manage, "please let them know that we have some cleanup work to do first. I'll get with them as soon as possible."

"I've already told them that, babycakes."

"Thank you."

"They said to make it quick."

CHAPTER 5

I snapped on a fresh pair of shoes, after wrangling the old ones into a bag, being careful not to touch the goop-covered one. I wasn't going to wear them again because I knew what they'd been through.

"You think I should donate these?" I asked Rachel.

"Seriously?"

"What? I'd have them cleaned first."

"Would *you* wear them knowing where they'd been, even after having them cleaned?"

I frowned at her. "Obviously not, or I wouldn't be considering donating them."

"My point, exactly." She looked back at the shoes. "I'd say burn them."

She was probably right, but the idea was silly. It's not like they had any weird infection on them that would cause the next person who wore them to turn into a zombie.

"Shit," I said, feeling the blood fall from my face.

"What?"

"You don't think the blood or goop or whatever it was on my shoes is infectious, do you?"

She tilted her head. "What do you mean?"

"I've been touching that shoe," I answered, pointing. "So did Felicia. Are we going to turn into…"

"Don't say it," she interrupted before I could continue my thought. "You can't possibly believe that."

"You've seen the movies, Rachel."

"Hollywood, Ian." She had her arms crossed again. Why she ever uncrossed them around me was a mystery. "There's no evidence that a zombie bite or zombie…juice is going to cause you or anyone to become a zombie."

"But you don't know that."

We were both silent for a few moments, staring at the bag in the back of the car. Sure it was ridiculous to think that this was some kind of infectious thing, even if most of the movies and books said that was the case. But what if there was something to it? Most stories that we read are based on facts, right? Tales about vampires, werewolves, pixies, and so on were all based on reality. Loosely based, sure, but legends are rarely grown out of nothing.

"Burn them," she said again, looking less sure of herself. She obviously caught on to the fact that I was staring at her incredulously. "What?"

"You just said…"

"I know what I said, Ian." Her arms tightened as a worried look crested her face. "Burn them."

"Yeah."

"Actually," she said, unfolding her arms and pushing me back, "I have an even better idea."

A light energy rolled out of her hands and levitated the bag out of the car. She moved it until it was on the grass and then blasted it with a fireball. It made a whooshing sound and disappeared.

"You okay?" yelled Jasmine from her spot near the rest of the gang.

21

JOHN P. LOGSDON & CHRISTOPHER P. YOUNG

"Yeah," I called back. "Just…uh…getting rid of my shoes."

There was no response. Either they thought we were nuts or they agreed with our level of caution. Probably a little of both.

"What about me and Felicia?" I said, reminding Rachel that we'd both touched the shoes.

She began walking back toward the others. "I could flame you both like I did your shoes, but I'm guessing you'd rather wait to see if symptoms appear."

"Nice."

When we approached the rest of the crew, Griff was walking along the opened graves.

Rick Portman from the supernatural morgue would be here any minute to help clean things up. If Lydia gave him the full lowdown, he and his crew would have some type of hazmat suits on. At least, I hoped they would. Until we knew more about this zombie stuff, precaution would be rule one.

"What's he doing?" Rachel asked Chuck.

"Counting the graves."

"Why?"

"To be certain that we have a one-to-one ratio," Griff replied before Chuck could. "If there are more graves then there are bodies, that will mean…"

"That some of them got away," I finished for him.

"Precisely so," Griff stated with a stiff nod.

Then he let out a slow breath. The look on his face spelled trouble. Everyone knew it.

"How many?" I said, trying to keep a measure of calm.

"Seven."

"Swell." I paused. "Maybe they all froze up because you shut off the magic light show?"

"You saw those above ground were still moving, Chief," noted Chuck.

"True."

We all started scanning the area, hoping to spot them in the yard. Even with my enhanced vision, I couldn't spot any of the damn things nearby. I zoomed as far as I could and swept the area again.

There was one across the street. It was heading toward the housing complex across Eldorado. I couldn't have that.

"There's one," I said as I took off running at it.

"Make sure it's a zombie before you fire at it, Chief," Felicia called after me.

I hopped the fence in full stride and bolted right at the creature, pulling out Boomy in the process. Within a few feet of it, I heard the wheezing and coughing that was the trademark of all zombies in the movies.

Just as I was about to pop a bullet into its head, it turned and looked at me.

"Don't shoo...*hic*...shoot," said a man who looked to have seen better years.

It was a hobo who was clearly shitfaced. He reeked of soured booze and a lack of proper bathing. And even though I had a gun pointed at him, he clung to his bottled wine like it was his most prized possession.

Rachel caught up a moment later, hands aglow.

"It's just a bum," I said, panting.

"That's not ni...*hic*...nice," the guy said as if affronted. "I used to be som...somebody, you know?"

"Right," I said with a weak smile. "Sorry, pops. Thought you were someone else."

"Sto...*hic*...story of my life."

He continued on his way while singing some song about lost love and loneliness.

"Well, that was close," said Rachel. "Obviously we're going to need to vet our zombies before just outright killing them."

"Seems so." I glanced back at the cemetery and opened the full channel on the connector. "False alarm. Was just an old drunk guy. Is there any way to track these damn things?"

"Not that I know of."

"Well, then let's start combing the area. We have seven to pick up before they start biting people and turning everyone into zombies!"

CHAPTER 6

"*I*t doesn't work like that," said Griff after Rachel and I rejoined the group.

I turned and looked at him. "What doesn't work like what?"

"The myth regarding a zombie bite resulting in the one bitten turning into a zombie."

"Oh, right." I nodded and then squinted. "It doesn't?"

"No. In fact, the term zombie is rather boorish." Sometimes his uppityness was annoying. He was wealthy, yes, but so was I, and you didn't hear me talking condescendingly all the time. Sometimes, certainly, but that was a requirement of being uber rich. To be fair, though, Griff was from old money. Very old. He came from an age where drinking tea with your pinky sticking out was considered civilized. "What we saw here were merely reanimated corpses who had been instilled with a desire to attack."

"Right," I said, rubbing my chin seriously. "So, you mean they're...*zombies*?"

Griff sighed.

25

"Whatever we call them," said Jasmine as she walked between Griff and me, "we need to round them up before they attack someone."

"True," said Griff and I in unison.

A slew of white vans pulled up, signaling that Rick Portman and his cleanup crew had arrived.

Portman was a werebear. You could almost tell by looking at him in his normal state because he was a big bear of a man with bushy brown hair and a matching beard. Plus, he was the kind of guy who lumbered when he walked. His crew were all donning protective suits, but Portman wasn't the type who bothered with things like that.

"Everyone split up," I commanded my team. "They couldn't have gotten too far. Remember there are seven of them. We get seven and we're done."

Griff and Chuck took off toward South Eastern, and Jasmine and Felicia headed to Robindale.

"Dex?" called out Portman as Rachel and I took the Eldorado side and combed our way toward the housing development at the end of the cemetery grounds.

"Hey, Portman," I said, pausing while Rachel continued on. "Can't really chat. Got a bunch of zombies on the loose."

"Zombies, eh?" He'd said it in such a way that made me think he thought I'd been drinking. I pointed at the corpses littering the ground. "Oh, wow. There *are* zombies. Lydia told me that, but I thought maybe she'd had a software upgrade to add in a sense of humor or something."

"That's what I thought!"

He eyed the area worriedly. "Need any help?"

"If you want to take a few people and go up to that corner," I said, pointing, "we've got seven on the loose."

"Sweet." He rubbed his hands excitedly. "I usually don't get them until *after* they're dead. It'll be fun to take some out beforehand for once."

"That's...disturbing." I then raised an eyebrow. "You do realize that they're already dead, technically speaking?"

"Thanks for ruining it for me, Dex."

With that we split apart and took off running. Rachel was already a good distance in front of me, clearly having decided not to sit through my stirring discourse with Portman. I caught up to her quickly.

"Anything?"

"Nope."

"Chief," said Chuck through the connector, "Griff and I just dropped two of them. They were heading in from the corner of Eldorado and South Eastern."

So those *were* zombies that I saw when I'd turned the corner after the taco joint.

Right?

"You *did* verify they were zombies first, yes?"

"They were most assuredly reanimated corpses," Griff answered.

I made a face in the air, mocking Griff, but simply replied, "Excellent."

"Straight ahead," Rachel said, holding out a hand to slow me down. "Do you see them?"

There were three forms dragging themselves across the dirt field. This section of the cemetery hadn't been greened up with grass yet. King David was apparently growing their business, though, because the dirt looked to be packed down nicely. I guess when it came to cemeteries, people were just dying to get in there.

"Why are we slowing down?" I asked, thinking that maybe Rachel had some interesting plan in mind.

"I uh..." She stopped and looked at me. "Habit, I guess. Sneaking up on the bad guys and all that, you know?"

"Gotcha." Then I had an idea. "Any chance you could cast

a nifty spell that causes roots to come up out of the ground and hold them in place?"

She merely blinked at me.

"What?"

"Roots?" she mostly snorted. "Wizards do crap like that. You know I don't."

"It doesn't have to be roots, exactly, Rachel," I retaliated. Why was everyone so particular? "My point is to find *some* way to hold them in place so they can't attack us."

She sighed and said, "Fine." She waved her hands around for a second and launched a white orb at their legs. They instantly fell down. Then they turned and started crawling toward us. "There."

"That was pretty effective. Why didn't you do this before when we were fighting a bunch of them?"

"Because I didn't think about it."

"It just seems that it would make sense…"

She pointed at the oncoming zombies. "Any chance you could shut up and shoot those damn things?"

I casually leveled my gun and placed three bullets into three craniums.

They stopped crawling.

"Boy, that sure was a lot simpler than when they…"

Something slammed in to me from behind, knocking Boomy from my hands and throwing me facedown in the dirt. The smell of rotted flesh was nearly overwhelming until my world became a searing force of pain and anguish.

The thing had bitten me.

CHAPTER 7

"*J*an," Rachel yelled as I writhed around on the ground, "it did *not* bite you."

I stopped my groaning and looked up at her. She was leaning over with a face that mixed concern and disbelief. It reminded me of a time when we used to date and I asked how she'd felt about handcuffs in the bedroom.

"It didn't?" I asked, hoping that she was right.

"No."

I felt at my neck, expecting the worst, but there was no gouge. I was covered in slime or something, but there were no holes in my flesh that I could make out.

"Then what the hell did I feel?" I asked. "It hurt like hell."

"I cast a targeted blast of energy and blew its head off *before* it could bite you."

"Oh…thanks." I sat up and nearly vomited at the realization of what constituted the slime that was covering me. To be sure, though, I asked the question I really didn't want to ask. "Are you saying that this is brain goop all over me?"

"Yep."

"Nasty!" I began pulling it out of my hair and scooping it off my face, throwing it all on the ground while fighting the urge to decorate my second pair of shoes with bile.

Then I paused.

Something wasn't adding up. If Rachel blew the thing's head off before it could bite me, what was that searing pain I'd felt? Maybe it *did* bite me and she'd just healed it? She wasn't a healer like Serena was, but she had a spell or two that she could use in a pinch.

"If I wasn't bitten," I said as my thoughts continued racing, "why did that hurt so bad?"

"Hmmm?" she said while looking around the area.

"My neck."

"What about it?"

She was acting too innocent. Something was going on. I'd known her long enough to tell when she was hiding something from me.

"Rachel?"

"I think I see one over there," she said, ignoring me. "No, that's Portman."

"Rachel?" I became a little more insistent.

"We should probably head down…"

"Rachel!"

She jolted. "What?"

"Why did that hurt so bad?"

"Why did what hurt so bad?"

"You're stalling," I said with a sharp look.

And then it hit me. I reached for my neck again and noticed that the flesh was a little softer in one spot than in the rest. That only happened when…

"Holy shit," I said, opening my eyes in shock. "You shot me!"

"Hmmm?"

"Son of a bitch." I was beside myself at this point. "When

you fired at that zombie, it went straight through and took a chunk out of my neck."

She tilted her head and squinted, peering in to study the covered-up wound. "It did?"

"Unbelievable."

It was a rare thing for Rachel to screw up. I did it all the time, and she pointed it out in equal measure, but for her to foul things up somehow was like finding a diamond at the bottom of the ocean. It didn't happen very often.

Then I felt a sense of horror. "Did zombie bits get into the cut? Oh shit! Have I got zombie bits in me?"

"Relax, Ian," she stated firmly. "I made sure all the zombie bits were out before…"

She stopped herself and turned white. Then she opened and closed her mouth a few times, clearly seeking the right words. Finally, she slumped over.

I took a deep breath, trying to maintain my composure. It wasn't easy. I had no doubt she'd actually got all the zombie bits out, and I believed Griff when he said that there was no "infection" or anything related to being bitten by a zombie or by touching zombie juice, but it was still beyond disgusting.

It was my turn to cross my arms at her.

"Remember a couple weeks back when I screwed up and you were kidnapped by a werewolf?" I asked pointedly.

Her eyes grew dark for a moment and then she tore away her gaze and nodded.

"We're even," I stated sternly. "And I want it noted that you were never injured or anything when you were taken during my mistake. You also didn't get covered in werewolf parts." I started walking away, but stopped and yelled, "Oh yeah, and I didn't shoot you!"

"So much for 'we're even,'" she replied, tailing me like a scorned puppy.

"Hey, Chief," Felicia said through the connector, "Jasmine

and I didn't spot any on our route, but Portman just dragged one back. Looks like there are still four missing."

"No," I replied, giving Rachel a glare. "We got lucky and dropped four out here. Three were crawling about and one attacked."

"You guys okay?"

"We're peachy." I cleared my throat. "Have Griff do a recount, just to make sure. Also, Portman should send a few of his team to collect the ones out here."

"You got it, Chief."

The walk back was mostly quiet, except for the sounds of vehicles passing by.

There was a time, long before I was the chief, where Rachel and I would take late night strolls together. Not in a cemetery, of course. Usually it was at a park or even just down the strip. Things were different now, though. They had to be.

"You going to tell everyone?" she asked.

"Would you?"

"No."

"Liar."

We got back and everyone gave me the once-over. It was obvious that I looked dreadful. Hell, I *felt* dreadful.

"What happened to you?" said Felicia.

"Nothing," I replied, glancing at Rachel. "Nothing at all."

Portman reached into his van, pulled out a towel, and threw it at me. I studied the rest of his crew. They were all wiping remnants of something off their person. I assumed it had to do with how they'd destroyed the poor zombie they'd found.

"All the bodies are indeed accounted for," Griff announced, "assuming your count was accurate."

"There were four," Rachel confirmed.

"There you have it, then."

I went to hand the towel back to Portman, but he pointed at a barrel that was half full of them already. I dumped it in there.

"You need our help here, Portman?"

"Nah, all set. This was a fun night, Dex. Thanks for the invite."

"Yeah," I replied with a sniff. "It was a real hoot." I then turned to my team and added, "Let's get back to base. We've obviously got a new problem on our hands."

CHAPTER 8

*T*he Directors were already waiting when I entered the meeting room, which was accessed via the door at the back of my office.

There were four of them on the panel. I could only see flashes or basic shadows of them in the dim lighting, and the moment they pulled away my memory of their faces faded. It was like speaking with apparitions.

Silver, the representative for the vampires, opened the conversation. "We've been told that reanimated corpses appeared off the strip, but we don't know any further details. What have you learned?"

Right, so no pleasantries today.

"Not much yet, sir," I replied with an equally businesslike tone. "We arrived on the scene, were subsequently attacked, killed them, in a manner of speaking, and are now working through how this all happened."

"But you must have some idea?" grumbled Zack, the werewolf rep.

"Griff..." I started and then decided to go formal instead.

"I mean, Officer Benchley, suggested that it has to do with necromancy."

"This is obvious," noted O. He was the top-dog for the Crimson Focus Mages. Usually he was one of the more cordial Directors of the bunch, but today he seemed just as snippy at the rest of them. "The very fact that they came out of the ground denotes necromancy, Mr. Dex."

"I'm aware of that, sir," I said, fighting to maintain my cool. It wasn't easy considering that I still carried zombie juice on my person. I took a deep breath. "What we know is that bodies crawled out of the ground and that's highly unusual."

"No shit," said EQK, offering his two cents.

"Officer Benchley found a magical power line that was moving across the ground," I continued, ignoring the Vegas Pixies representative. "As it crossed the graves, it reanimated those inside. They came up with the desire to attack us."

"Your team specifically?" Silver asked.

If anything, it seemed like *me* specifically. The zombies hadn't gone into attack-mode until I'd arrived, after all. Still, there wasn't enough data to jump to that conclusion yet.

"That I don't know," I replied, keeping my expression even. "We were the only ones in the immediate area at the time. Or at least the only ones required to stay and fight the things."

"If Officer Benchley spotted a combing light," O mused, "then the necromancer had to have been nearby."

"We didn't see anybody," I said and then I remembered the hobo. It wasn't much, but in the essence of full-disclosure, I said, "Wait, scratch that. There *was* an old guy walking across the street. He was just a drunk...I think."

"Probably not," O stated. "Did he look sickly and small?"

"Yeah, but most drunks in this town look like that." I

licked my lips and suddenly regretted it. The taste of zombie juice is not exactly pleasant. "You think that was the guy?"

"There's no way to be certain without having the ability to speak with him," O answered after a moment, "but it would seem likely. People who dabble in necromancy tend to shrink over time. I've seen large men morph into a fraction of their normal selves."

Damn it. I had the guy right in my hands and let him go. To be fair to me, though, he was a pretty decent actor. Assuming it wasn't actually just some drunk. The real necro could have been anywhere.

"What is your plan?" asked Zack, jolting me from my thoughts.

"My crew is working on it now." I didn't know if Rachel or Jasmine knew much about necromancy or not, but it seemed that Griff had the topic well in hand. "I have Officer Benchley heading up the research."

"Wise," said O. "He's dealt with this before."

"Before?" I raised an eyebrow at that. "What do you mean he's dealt with this before?"

"He means it's not the first time this has happened, you boob," EQK explained.

I glanced toward the pixie and then back at the place where O sat. "When?"

"Many times over the years, Mr. Dex," answered O. "It's an art that we in the mage community have shunned. We've gone to great lengths to eradicate it and all of its users."

"Good work," said Silver.

"I note and accept your sarcasm, Silver," O said without inflection. "It's not a simple thing to pin down those with ill will, as I'm sure your vampire brethren can attest."

There was a pause, and Silver replied, "True." His voice sounded heavy.

"It's the same with werewolves," admitted Zack. "We have many tarnishes on our historical record."

While I couldn't see the panel, I had the distinct feeling that everyone had turned to stare at EQK. They'd all owned up to their particular lot having nefarious sorts among their numbers and now they were looking to the pixie to join the crowd.

My assumption was verified when EQK said, "Screw you guys. We don't raise the dead or bite people or go running around marking our territory by pissing on trees." There was a light growl from Zack. "Sorry, dudes, but pixies just aren't like you warped fuckers."

CHAPTER 9

*M*y crew was already in the conference room when I returned from the precinct showers. I snagged a quick sandwich from the vending machine directly across from them and wolfed it down.

I was cleaned up, moderately fed, and feeling like I belonged in the world again.

As I walked into the room I found that Warren and Serena had joined the fun, along with Turbo. None of them were street officers, per se. They all worked at the PPD, of course, and Warren and Serena had enhanced genetics, though the horny side-effect didn't seem to impact Warren at all. I used to praise anything that would listen regarding how the horny gene impacted Serena though. Ah, those were the days.

Turbo was a pixie who managed all of our technological needs. Everything from software to hardware, if it needed building or fixing, Turbo was our guy. He had coke-bottle glasses and wore a little police officer uniform, including a badge and everything. It wasn't really protocol for the PPD, but it seemed to make him happy. He was also one of the fortunate ones who didn't need genetic enhancements.

Warren was our only wizard on staff. He had that hippie thing going with the long straggly hair and matching beard. It wasn't gray, though, and he wasn't old, but he did have leathery skin that marked him as having spent too many days on the beach.

Serena handled forensics, which put her in the limelight alongside Griff. If there was any one person I could lay with for all eternity, it'd be Serena. I don't mean that in a spiritual way. While she was nice enough, we were compatible in the sack only. Roleplaying, specifically. She played the role of succubus and I played the role of lucky guy who got to be with her while she played the role of succubus.

… back when I wasn't chief.

I sighed and got my head back in the game.

"What's the word, people?" I asked as I moved to the head of the table.

"I've been doing some research alongside of Serena," answered Griff, "and we are planning to return to the King David Cemetery so that she can study the area in greater detail."

Serena nodded and added, "I'm going to try and pick up the necro's trail."

"Right, uh, about that." I coughed and rubbed my nose. "My guess is that he was crossing Eldorado after we'd dropped the majority of the zombies."

"What?" said Rachel with a look of shock. "You mean the old guy?"

"Exactly what I mean. O pointed it out when I was meeting with the Directors."

Griff leaned forward. "Interesting."

He looked like a man who could use a nice long nap. All of the mages did, in fact. That was one of the drawbacks of

JOHN P. LOGSDON & CHRISTOPHER P. YOUNG

their profession. They got tired a lot faster than the rest of us.

"Looks to me like you could all use a little rest."

There was no argument.

"Lydia," I called out, "do you know if Portman got everything squared away at the graveyard?"

"He checked in about fifteen minutes ago, sugar. Said everything was back to normal."

"Good. What about Paula? She's still in the dark, yes?"

Paula Rose was the head of the local company that handled public relations for the PPD. The company was called The Spin and they had the unenviable job of making all of the crazy junk the supernatural community did look like standard Vegas happenings to the normals. The problem was that she only had one easy way out of any oddity, and that was to say it was a new show in the works. People bought it because they were mostly drunk when seeing things out of the ordinary. Paula hated using that line, though. She wanted some other type of spin on at least a few things.

"I haven't spoken with her."

"Good."

Good for me, mostly. Paula and I used to date back in the day. It didn't work out. That was my fault, of course. She couldn't keep up with my libido. Very few can. I glanced again at Serena, knowing full well that she *could*. Fact is that I'm not the cheating type, so I'd broken up with her, explaining it was better for me to do that than to become unfaithful. She hadn't taken it well and it made for a shaky working relationship. It had improved over the years, but I still went out of my way to avoid her whenever possible.

"Any reports coming from other grave sites?" Rachel asked.

"No, Ms. Cress," Lydia replied in the robotic voice she

reserved for the rest of my crew. I always found this funny because it irritated Rachel so much. "Currently everything is clear."

"We should probably still do some checking around," Felicia suggested. "Just in case."

Everyone was nodding at that, except Chuck who was busily reading something.

"Reading up on Zombies, Chuck?

Chuck turned the book to reveal a bluish cover with two dudes looking smokin' hot, fierce, and snappily dressed.

"Ah, right." I coughed lightly, recalling his relationship with Griff. "Not on work time, please."

"It's a Montague & Strong Detective Agency novel, you idiot," said Rachel while shaking her head at me. "I have all of them."

"Oh, sorry."

How was I supposed to know? And what made Rachel assume I was being insensitive anyway? I *was*, but she didn't know that.

I glanced up at her and remembered how long we'd worked together. She could spot me from a mile away…. A thought struck me.

"Turbo," I said, leaning in, "what are the chances of you being able to create a way for us to spot these things?"

His eyes darted around the room. "Montague & Strong Detective Agency novels?"

"No," I said, grimacing at him. "I'm talking about zombies. It'd be great if there was some way that we could know if something was dead before we killed it." Turbo squinted at me. I sought to clarify. "Can you create a way for us to know who is a zombie and who isn't?"

"Only matters if they *are* one, right?" he asked. "Why do you care to know who isn't?"

Working with techies wasn't my thing. They were a bit

too logical for me. I asked them to build something based off of a general idea and I either got the run around, the make-Ian-look-like-an-idiot routine, or the "Sure, Chief, but it'll take three weeks to get it done."

"You're right," I said with some effort. "My mistake. Can you create a way for us to be able to spot zombies?"

"I suppose I could," he said while pacing back and forth on the little desk he'd been standing on. He was moving so fast that he was nearly a blur. Finally, he stopped and said, "It'll take me about three weeks."

"We don't have three weeks," I replied, playing the part I'd learned over my years of working with him.

"I could do it faster, but with speed you lose quality, or money, or both."

At least we'd progressed to argument number two more rapidly than usual.

"All we need is to spot the zombies accurately," I stated. "It doesn't have to be pretty and it doesn't need a lot of bells and whistles. The tech simply has to allow us to identify zombies. That's it."

"Hmmm," he said, resuming his pacing. "It can be done, certainly. I think so, anyway. I could run patterns against breathing, pulse detection, and a number of other items to verify that the person is alive."

"I thought you said it didn't matter if they were alive." I couldn't help giving him a dig. "It only mattered if they were dead."

"True, Chief, and well done," Turbo said, looking impressed, "but in order to see if the person is dead, I first have to rule out them being alive."

I took a deep breath. "How long, Turbo? And three weeks isn't the answer I'm looking for, either."

"You're sure you don't want anything fancy?"

"I'm sure."

He tapped his little foot on the desk while adjusting his policeman's cap. "I only ask because usually you want these things really fast and then you complain that they're not very effective because they need some fancy bits thrown in."

He was right. If I wasn't specific enough, I'd get something ridiculous, but if I was too specific, it'd never get completed. A vision of him delivering a zombie detector that was the size of a refrigerator passed before my eyes.

"Okay, fair enough," I said finally. "We have to be able to easily carry the device. It can't be overly bulky and it would be best if it were hands-free so that we can still fire our weapons and do magic."

"Good, good," he said as his eyes grew wide. "Yes, I can see it now." He was doing what appeared to be calculations in the air. "No, no, don't want to do that. But if…"

"Sorry to interrupt," I said with a smile. He paused. "Maybe you can work this out with the help of Lydia?"

"Yes, yes! I'll do that."

"Try not to take too long," I called after him as he zipped out of the room. "We may need these things very soon."

I hoped that wasn't true, but since that little old drunk guy was likely our necromancer, and seeing as how I hadn't taken him into custody the first time around, the likelihood was that we were going to be running into a lot more zombies before too long.

"All right, gang," I said finally, "let's get to it."

43

CHAPTER 10

*R*achel and I hopped into the Aston Martin and started canvasing cemeteries. It wasn't all that thrilling, but a little downtime was cool with me right about now.

Jasmine and Felicia took the south side of town.

Since Griff and Serena were heading back to King David, Chuck had taken Warren along with him. While that probably wasn't the best partnership in the history of the paranormal police department, Warren could serve as backup if given time. He had sent that weakening spell at Reese a few weeks back, after all.

"So anyway," Rachel said as we cruised down the strip, "sorry about shooting you in the neck."

If you knew Rachel as well as I did, your jaw would be hitting the floor right now. It was not in her DNA to apologize for anything. She must have really felt terrible.

"It happens," I replied with a shrug, trying not to make a big deal out of it. Her learning to say she was sorry about stuff could be a good thing, after all. "I suppose I never formally apologized for getting you kidnapped."

"Nope."

Trying to mirror her method so that she'd feel comfortable, I said, "Yeah, well, my bad."

She patted my hand. "That was very heartfelt, Ian. Honestly, I nearly shed tears."

So much for that.

At least we were back on "normal" terms with each other. Even though we could no longer do the boom-boom, as it were, Rachel had been my partner on the force for a long time. While I'd never admit it to her directly, she was the most important person in my life. She had my back and I had hers...when we weren't shooting each other and getting each other kidnapped anyway. We needed to stay tight and stick together.

I was about to flip on the radio but decided to keep the dialog going instead.

"Meet with Dr. Vernon this week?" I asked.

"Not yet." She groaned. "Hate that part of the job."

"Me, too." It was probably a mistake, but I decided to open up. If nothing else, it'd put the awkward apology phase behind us. "This time she told me that I was struggling with an inferiority complex or something."

Rachel started nodding. "Yeah, I can see that."

"What?" I glanced over to see that she was smiling mischievously. "Bitch." She giggled some more. "Anyway, before we got down to me laying on the couch and all that, she started asking me about my weapon."

"The Admiral?" Rachel said with a sense of surprise.

"Not *that* weapon," I replied slowly, recalling Rachel's pet name for my *other* weapon, and finding it quite interesting that after five years under the "no contact" rule, she remembered it too. "I'm talking about my gun."

"Ohhhh, right." The awkward apology phase had morphed into the awkward mentioning-her-pet-name-for-my-junk moment. She cleared her throat. "Sorry. Go on."

It was difficult to keep my gaze on the road because I wanted to turn and seriously frown at her.

I took a deep breath and jumped on to West Oakely. I've been in Vegas for most of my adult life, but it wasn't like I stopped off at graveyards much, so whenever the GPS chimed I had to spin the wheel.

"Anyway," I continued while thinking the idea of sharing was getting dumber by the second, "I'd taken out Boomy, removed the mag, and set it on the table."

"Okay?"

"Well, Dr. Vernon took one look at it and that's when the inferiority stuff became her angle for the day."

"Ah, I see. You walked in, flopped your weapon on the table, she sees that its got more ridges and accents than your normal weapon, and she starts thinking that maybe you're starting to feel that your normal weapon just isn't good enough."

It was said deadpan.

"Nice," I said with a sigh. "Try to open up and this is what I get."

She laughed even louder. "That's what she said."

"Oh, come on! You're being…"

"Ian?" Jasmine chimed in over the connector.

I gave another sharp look at Rachel, who was still in giggle mode. "Yes, Jasmine?"

"We've got bogies at Bunkers Eden Vale Memorial."

"Shit." Time to get serious. I flipped the connector and read off the cemetery name so that the GPS could find the fastest route. "How many?"

"Hard to say," Jasmine answered, "but definitely more than a few."

"On our way," I replied while making a u-turn. "Lydia, can you get the rest of the crew out to Bunkers Ed…"

"Already informed everyone, sweetums," she interrupted. "They're all en route. And before you ask, Mr. Portman has also been notified. As per our previous discussion, I'll wait for your 'okay' before I inform Ms. Rose."

"You're the best, Lydia."

"You have no idea."

Rachel's humor had changed over to disgust at that interchange, which I found terrific. Jealousy? Maybe. Annoyance that Lydia didn't give her the same friendly treatment I got? Definitely.

"Just out of curiosity," Rachel said in a voice that spelled trouble, "have you told Dr. Vernon about how desperately you want to have sex with the force's A.I.?"

"Of course not," I answered before realizing that I'd just admitted I wanted to bone Lydia.

I glanced over to see Rachel grinning again. "Too easy."

CHAPTER 11

*T*he Bunkers Eden Vale Memorial cemetery sat directly across from the Palm Downtown cemetery. But from what I could tell, only Bunkers was having a "crawl out" extravaganza on graves.

"Notice anything strange about this?" I asked Rachel as I slowed the car at the corner of North Las Vegas Boulevard and East Searles Avenue.

"You mean besides the zombies walking around over there?"

"Exactly," I said while pointing to the opposite side of the road. "There are *none* walking over there."

She did a double-take. "Huh."

"I also didn't see any back at Woodlawn, but that place is much larger than Bunkers so maybe they're just well-hidden."

There were multiple cemeteries in this area, but it looked like only Bunkers was facing a corpse exodus. This was probably due to the old man having only so much time and power, but I wasn't a pro when it came to his selected profession. Seeing that Rachel's response was simply "huh," I assumed she wasn't highly versed in necromancy either.

Jasmine and Felicia were still sitting in the Camaro when we pulled up. I saw no sign of the rest of the team, but seeing that we'd been the closest when the call came in that made sense.

"They're just milling around again?" I said through the window to Felicia. "Wonder what they're waiting for?"

"No idea, Chief," Felicia answered. "Pretty damn freaky if you ask me, though."

"Yeah."

I pulled ahead of her and parked.

Boomy was already loaded up with fresh rounds and I had multiple mags at the ready. Rachel had gone into a light trance, which meant she wasn't planning to go in cold like she had back at King David's. That was good.

I didn't want to get too close to the zombies until everyone got here, but I did want a better view of the area. Primarily, I was looking to spot our drunk old man again. A famous Who song about not getting fooled again sprang to mind.

"Stay here," I said to Rachel. "I'm going to scout the area for Shitfaced Fred."

She opened one eye. "Who?"

"That's what I'm calling our fake drunkard."

"Why?"

I shrugged. "He looked like he was pretty wasted and I like the name Fred. Does it really matter?"

"Right," she replied, closing her eyes again. "Be careful."

I stepped out of the car and motioned Jasmine and Felicia to stay put. They didn't like it, but I didn't want to put them in jeopardy unless absolutely necessary. It wasn't easy being the boss.

While I couldn't see the entirety of the graveyard, mostly

due to the trees, it looked like there were fewer open graves than we'd faced before. It was also good that the area wasn't immediately surrounded by housing. It'd be a long walk for any of these dead guys to slip into a house during late-night movie time.

That begged the question why our necromancer was attacking in the outskirts. Was he just practicing for something bigger? I hoped not, but so far I had very little to go on.

Speaking of Shitfaced Fred, I didn't see him anywhere. Of course he could have been on top of one of the buildings, hiding in a tree, or completely gone. For all I knew, he might have even been masquerading as a tombstone.

"Chief," Felicia said through the connector, "Chuck and Warren just pulled up. Griff and Serena are going to hit the access street on the other side and close in that way."

"Good," I whispered while continuing my study.

Apparently my whisper didn't go unnoticed. The air went still. The crunching of feet on grass and the moaning of reanimated corpses ceased.

I'd been spotted and all eyes were on me.

I gulped.

A bloodcurdling scream ripped from the zombie closest to me. It was obviously a signal so that all his buddies could join him in ripping me to shreds, but it sounded like a naked wrestler learning what yarn feels like when a playful cat's around.

"Shit," I yelled in return as I stuck a bullet between the creature's eyes.

It fell backward with a glorious thud, and then pushed itself right back up.

"What the fuck?"

I fired again. It got up again.

"Chief," Felicia called through the connector, "the zombies are on the move."

"Don't I know it," I replied while running at full-tilt back to the cars, unleashing Boomy at every head that came too close to me. But it wasn't stopping them. "Shooting them in the head isn't working."

"What?"

"You heard me, Felicia. It's not working. We need some magic on these guys or something."

"Aim for their hearts," Jasmine suggested.

"Why?"

"Why not?"

"Good point."

I turned my head and fired at the closest one. It dropped and didn't move. So the necro had moved the kill point to the heart? Great. He was working out ways to make his little zombie army tougher to kill.

"That worked," I said, spinning my head back and running square into the chest of a rather large corpse.

We both hit the ground as Boomy went flying. I really needed to invest in a tether for that damn gun.

I was lying on top of the corpse, looking down into its lifeless eyes.

It clearly wasn't fond of this arrangement, because it made a very odd wheezing sound and threw me up in the air. For a dead guy, he was incredibly strong. I landed on a rock, which didn't feel all that great, but this was no time for pain. Besides, I'd heal fast enough.

I rolled up and spun to see something I really didn't expect.

The zombie who had just liberated me from his person was standing still, gurgling as the rest of the corpses came to a halt around him. The mass of dead stood a couple of paces back from the big guy, seemingly curious about how the scene would unfold. They were staring so intently it was like they had seats to the event of the century. Honestly, if there'd been a popcorn vendor walking around, he'd have made a killing.

But that wasn't what worried me most.

What had me on edge was the fact that the zombie boss was holding Boomy and he was pointing it at my chest.

CHAPTER 12

*N*ow you would think that my first reaction would have been to duck, dive out of the way, run like hell, or all of the above. But instead, I stood there with my arms up while thinking, "Do I know this guy?"

I whispered "idiot" to myself on behalf of Rachel, since she wasn't around to do it for me.

"Now you die, vampire," gurgled the zombie.

"You can speak?" I said as my eyes fought against bursting from my head. Then I frowned at the realization of what he'd just said. "I'm *not* a vampire."

He paused and looked me over. In fact, the entire corpse crowd was looking me over, even those who only had eye sockets.

Then he lowered the gun slightly and tilted his head. "You're not?"

"No, and I honestly don't understand why everyone thinks I am." I put my hands on my hips. "I've got nothing against vampires, but I'm not one of them, and your assumption that I am is not cool. How would you like it if I called you a living, breathing person because I wasn't one hundred percent sure you were dead?"

That was clearly the wrong thing to say because all of their faces creased sinisterly. As if they didn't look scary enough already. How the hell was I to know that zombies weren't all that fond of being reminded they were dead?

The huge dead guy raised the gun up again and said, "Now, you die."

It was time to let gravity do its job. I fell straight down a split-second before he unleashed Boomy. I could survive a lot of things, but a 50-caliber hole in my chest wasn't one of them.

A wave of light smashed into his side before he could adjust his aim and try again. It knocked him over, causing Boomy to fly from his hands. Maybe *not* having a tether was a good thing, after all.

The rest of the dead spun to see where the source of the magic originated. It was Rachel and Jasmine, and they were on a tear.

Fireballs, lightning, ice, and all other sorts of mayhem flew from their fingers as Chuck and Felicia started plugging hearts with lead. Warren was nowhere to be seen, which either meant he'd stayed in the car or he was finding a safe place to cast a lengthy spell. I could definitely do with one of his void walls about now. Whether it would work on zombies or not, I couldn't say, but there'd be some catharsis in trying.

"Are you hit, Chief?" asked Felicia.

"I'm good," I replied while snapping up Boomy.

There was zombie juice all over it.

"What the…" I held it up. It dripped. "Son of a bitch."

Now I was pissed.

It was one thing to try and break me in half, or bite a hole in my neck, or throw me off a building, or run me over with a car, or even mistake me for a vampire. But shooting at me with my own gun while getting zombie juice all over it was just fucking wrong.

I went ballistic, firing Boomy off like it was our first date.

As an amalgamite, I was already fast, but when you pumped adrenaline into the mix, I was insanely speedy. No, I couldn't keep up with the likes of Turbo, but I wasn't far off.

My vision was tight and my arm steady. Magazines slipped in and out like they were on a high-tech production line. Every bullet hit its intended target without fail. Bodies dropped so quickly that it looked like a group of robots who had just had their collective power cut.

For every zombie my crew dropped, I took out three.

"Damn, Chief," Chuck said when it was all over, "maybe let us have a little fun too next time?"

"Huh?" was all I could reply before I dropped to a knee, feeling quite out of it. This tended to happen whenever I got a little overzealous.

Rachel rushed to my side and put her hand on my shoulder.

I instantly calmed, my heart slowing back to normal. It wasn't magic when she did that, it was familiarity. A sense of safety. The knowledge that my partner had my back.

"Thanks," I said before getting back up, my legs wobbly. "Are there more coming?"

"Griff shut down the necro's line," said Chuck, which meant his partner had informed him of such through the connector. "He's counting graves now."

I nodded. My strength and sense of self was steadying, but I'd still need a few minutes.

"So now we have to shoot them in the heart," I said finally.

"Or hit them there with magic, yeah," replied Jasmine. "It seems that fireballs were more effective than energy bursts.

At least for killing them." She paused. "It sounds so weird that we're having to 'kill' dead people."

Rachel looked at her. "I noticed the fireball thing, too, but over at King David's I recall energy blasts working better."

In response to that point, I subconsciously rubbed my neck where Rachel had taken a chunk out of me. Fortunately, she didn't look my way.

"I don't suppose anyone caught sight of Shitfaced Fred?"

Everyone looked at me, except Rachel.

"That's the nickname he's given to the necro," she explained. Then she held up a hand. "Before you ask, it's because the old guy was pretending to be drunk and Ian likes the name Fred."

They all shook their heads at me.

"I saw him," Warren said weakly through the connector. "Well, kind of."

"Where?" I asked, my senses returning.

His voice was shaky. "Near the cars."

We rushed back to find our resident wizard lying on the ground studying the stars. Was the necro up in the air? There weren't any trees about, so he couldn't have been on a branch or anything.

I followed Warren's line of vision to see if there was something specific he was looking at. "What are you doing?"

"Recovering from the knock to the head I received about twenty seconds after Chuck left the area," Warren whispered in response.

"Oh, damn." Chuck said, dropping down to help him. "Are you bleeding?"

"Probably."

Griff and Serena arrived a few seconds later and Serena moved to put her hands on Warren. With a smokin' hot vampire around to touch you when you needed healing, having a head injury wasn't so horrible.

"Unbelievable," Rachel said, obviously reading what was going through my brain.

"What?" I replied innocently.

"You're such a perv."

I blinked at her. "You say that like it's a bad thing."

CHAPTER 13

*G*riff's grave count matched up with the zombies we'd taken out, but we scoured the area for additional clues since it was obvious that our necromancer wasn't planning to go away anytime soon.

Portman and his crew already looked haggard from their work earlier that night, so they weren't exactly chipper about another round of burials.

"Any idea who the hell's doing this, Dex?" the big man asked as he wiped the dirt from his hands. He wasn't the type of boss who just stood around and watched. I respected that. "I'm not sure my team can handle another round of these without a sizable break."

"I hear you." I was still a bit achy myself. "You know the deal, though. Until we catch the guy, we're pretty much at his mercy."

"Yeah. Any leads?"

"Everyone's hunting for clues now. We know it's an old guy. Small. Looks kind of like a hobo."

Portman sighed. "Right. Well, I'll let you get back to it. We've still got a couple hours at best."

I nodded and walked off to where Griff and Serena were studying the grounds. They'd apparently found the spot where Fred was working from. I didn't see anything out of the ordinary, but I guessed there was magical residue Griff was picking up. He was busily casting spells over the area and Serena was analyzing the results.

Warren was sitting with his back against the car. He seemed to be working up some type of mojo, too.

"I see what they're doing," I said to Warren while pointing at Griff and Serena, "but what are you cooking up?"

"Tracking."

"That's a little too detailed for me, Warren," I said with a healthy dose of sarcasm. "How about you dumb it down a little?"

He looked up, confused. "Huh?"

"How is your spell going to track him?"

"Oh, sorry." He blinked a couple of times. "You know how dogs sniff a piece of a convict's clothes and then chase the scent?"

"Yes."

"Well, this is the same idea, but without the clothes." He then pointed at his shirt. "Before Fred knocked me out, he grabbed my shoulder. I guess for leverage. I don't know, honestly. But that left a signature."

I was slowly nodding. This could be quite useful for finding perps, assuming it was effective anyway. Actually, it was moments like this where I wanted to ask why we hadn't been using these little tricks to our advantage since day one. Warren's answer would have been "Nobody's ever knocked me on the head before" or something like that, though, so I let it go.

As my resident wizard continued on with his pygmy-like chanting, I listened in on Griff and Serena.

"He's definitely old power," Griff said. "If you look…" He suddenly stopped speaking and then keeled over.

Serena and I rushed to sit him back up.

His eyes were rolled up into his head and he was lightly convulsing.

"What the hell is going on?" I asked. "Is he having a stroke?"

"Give me a minute, Ian," Serena said calmly as her hands pulsed a very dim light.

Of all my agents, Serena was the most controlled. Her records showed that she was nearly as old as Griff, but just like him you'd never know it by looking at her. Anyone who didn't know her actual age would have placed her to be in her early thirties. Vampires tended to age well, after all. Serena had been taken down a different path than others on my crew. Instead of merely enhancing her speed and agility, things that were already prevalent in vampires, she got a bonus of the ability to heal. According to her personnel file she'd spent many years working in the field of medicine. It was clear that she had a knack for helping people, but she was also deadly when needed. This dichotomy made for the perfect succubus roleplaying partner, too. She could hurt you and then heal you.

Ah, the memories.

"The necro left a virus," she said as Griff's eyes rolled back to normal. She then glanced up at me. "We're dealing with something very new here, Ian."

I glanced around at the work that Portman and his crew were doing.

"Ya think?"

"Not just the zombies," she replied without inflection. "I'm talking about someone who is capable of weaving spells within spells."

"What happened?" Griff said a moment later while rubbing his temples.

Serena pushed his hands down and continued her therapy.

"Shitfaced Fred gave you a virus," I answered.

"Ah," Griff replied, closing his eyes again. "That explains the underlying elements I sensed before blacking out. This isn't good."

Seriously, sometimes I had to wonder about my team. Nonchalantly saying things like, "this isn't good" after being knocked to hell by an "underlying element" that was apparently code for "horrendously dangerous virus" was just irritating. Of course it wasn't good. If it was good, we wouldn't be out here trying to stop it.

I stood up as the rest of the crew came back.

Chuck moved to Griff's side immediately as Serena explained the virus situation, which put all the mages on edge. Even Warren seemed shaky about the proposition. I guess that made sense, seeing that his skill lay in the realm of magic, too.

"Do these viruses affect everyone or just magic users?" Felicia asked.

It was a great question.

"Only magic users," answered Griff.

"Phew," I said, wiping my brow.

"Don't forget that you can do magic, too, Ian," Rachel noted. "Not very well, but you still have the ability."

It was true that I could do magic. It was part of my amalgamiteness. But I tended to avoid it because I didn't have quite the control needed to do anything useful. Now and then I'd open a bottle of beer with a little spell or I'd maybe inflate a low tire, but I preferred destroying bad guys the old fashioned way. By using metallic projectiles flying from my gun. Plus, I wasn't anywhere near as adept with magic as my mages. My fireballs were about the size of pebbles. Imagine getting attacked by a single ember thrown at you every ten seconds and you'll see why I elected to use Boomy over magic.

"I don't suppose there's any correlation between how much power you wield and how effective that virus is?"

"Probably not," answered Griff as Chuck helped him back to his feet.

"Serena," Rachel said, "is it affecting you?"

"No. My healing stems from a different kind of magic than you're using. I feel the effects of the virus differently. It's passing through a filter with me."

That was good anyway. It was also good that Warren had been over by the car when Griff got zapped, or two of my magic users would have been laid out.

"I know this sounds dumb," I started, "but I don't suppose there's any type of virus protection we can do?"

"I have a few ideas," Griff replied, "but I'll need to work with Jasmine, Rachel, and Serena to get something put in place. We may have to reach out to other members of the Crimson Focus as well."

I couldn't help but feel a twinge of jealousy at that. Everyone had someone to call when they needed help with something relating to their profession or personal supernatural situation. Everyone except me, that is. Sure, I could yammer to Dr. Vernon, but she just nodded a lot, said "uh huh" in her judgmental way, and wrote things down in her book that couldn't have reflected all that well on me.

It'd be fantastic to find one other amalgamite in this world.

Preferably female.

"Guys," Warren called out, "I think I have something here."

CHAPTER 14

"*J*couldn't track him," Warren announced, "but I did learn something. Shitfaced Fred is a wizard."

I assumed that on the grand scheme of things, this was pertinent information. The nodding heads of my three mages claimed I was correct. Unfortunately, I needed context.

"I thought he was a necromancer," said Chuck before I could ask any questions.

"He's *practicing* necromancy," Griff replied as he tapped his chin, "but he's doing so more methodically than a mage would."

Wizards were notoriously slow. That was good, except that this guy seemed to be able to spin out a decent thread of magic at a rate that would make Warren's head spin. Obviously he had some way of speeding up the process.

"What are you talking about?" I asked.

"You've seen the differences, Chief," answered Warren. "I can't just cast spells whenever I feel like it. My magic requires study, planning, and detailed crafting. There are a few that I can do pretty quickly, sure, but anything of the level that Fred is doing would require a hell of a lot of prep time."

So I was right, but, again, Fred was zipping magic out like he was on crack.

"How much time are we talking here?"

Warren shrugged. "Days, if not weeks, Chief."

"But don't you see a problem with that?" I raised an eyebrow to convey that he really *should* be seeing a problem with his suggested timeline. He didn't. I clarified. "These zombies came up within hours of each other, not days or weeks."

"Oh, that's true." He licked his lips. "Not good."

"Definitely not good," agreed Rachel.

"Yes, I get that it's not good," I hissed. "We've got some drunk-looking, nutty wizard running around raising dead people; he's learning from how we defeat them and is tweaking them accordingly; and he's implemented a virus in his magic so that we get the shit knocked out of us if infected." They were all staring at me. "And now you're telling me that it should be taking him days or weeks to work out one of these attacks, but he's accomplished a couple of them within hours of each other. It's obviously *not good*, gang."

There was no response. They were clearly just as concerned about Shitfaced Fred as I was, but I tended to wear my emotions on my sleeve.

I took a deep breath.

"Sorry," I said finally. "I'm being a dick. We're just processing things differently is all." I looked down at my suit. "I've got zombie juice all over me again, Boomy is in need of a thorough cleaning, and that big-ass dead guy who tried to shoot me called me a vampire." I groaned. "You know how much that irritates me."

"It's okay, Chief," Warren replied.

"Wait," said Rachel after a second. "Are you saying that the dead guy *spoke* to you?"

I looked up. "Yeah, why?"

"It's weird, that's why. I didn't know zombies could speak."

The other mages were shaking their heads in agreement.

"Why wouldn't they be able to speak?" I asked, not really wanting to know the answer, but feeling like I had to know.

"Because..." Rachel started, but then stopped. "I don't know. It just seems odd."

I was okay with odd.

That's when I noticed that Griff was looking off into the distance. I was starting to dislike that about him. Every time he did it, something was wrong.

"From what I recall over past events," he said evenly, "reanimated corpses demonstrated no proclivity for an ability to speak."

Serena flicked a piece of grass from her sleeve. "Never in my dealings with them."

Okay, so it *was* a problem that zombies could talk. Besides it just being creepy, I mean. What I didn't know was *why* it was a problem.

"Let's cut to the chase here, guys," I said, looking from face to face. "Does it really matter if they can speak?"

"It might."

"Why do you say that, Warren?"

"Because it would mean that Fred can install power words in them."

I held up my hands and said, "The first one of you who says 'not good' is getting double-shifted for a week." They wisely remained quiet. "Now, what the hell is a power word, Warren?"

He looked suddenly put upon. "Whatever Fred wants it to

be, Chief. These things could heal themselves or others. They could cast fireballs of their own." His eyes were very wide. "He could essentially be raising a zombie army that has the capability to do magic."

I gulped and said, "Not good."

CHAPTER 15

The sun was starting to come up and that meant things were likely to die down for the night. Poor choice of words, I know.

Every now and then we'd get activity during the day, but it wasn't common. Besides, where subdivisions had a "neighborhood watch," we at the PPD had a "supernatural watch." There were members of the supernatural community who were always looking out for odd things to report. This typically resulted in a lot of bogus calls, but Lydia had learned to weed things out over the years.

The light on the cemetery showed that Portman and his crew had done an incredible job. A trained eye may have been able to spot if things were out of place, but I couldn't see anything off. To be fair, though, I wasn't hanging out in cemeteries all the time. Still, it was tight. There was no way Portman's gang had managed this manicuring through shovel work. There was magic involved, which made sense seeing that he had quite a few mages and wizards on his crew.

"All right everyone," I called out as Portman's line of

JOHN P. LOGSDON & CHRISTOPHER P. YOUNG

white vans drove away, "it's been a long night. We all need to get some rest because I'm sure we haven't seen the last of Fred."

There was no argument.

Rachel decided to hitch a ride back with Felicia and Jasmine since they were heading her way. Chuck and Griff lived in the same place, but they took Warren and Serena with them.

I cut down the strip and turned on to Jerry Lewis Way and into my condominium complex.

The Martin was a nice high rise that sat within walking distance of the Bellagio and the Aria. It was a classy joint with the standard palm trees deal on the drop-off/pick-up area. When I was looking for a place to hang my hat, there were many options, but I'd always thought of Dean Martin as the King of Cool. I never delved into the depths of his personal life or anything, but his TV and movie presence was enough for me. That meant that living in a building named after him suited me.

I threw my keys to the valet and pushed my way into the lobby, waved at the desk clerk, and jumped into the elevator.

My condo was modern with sleek lines and marble flooring. I could see most of downtown via the various windows that ran from one side of the place to the other, and the terrace was huge. Five bedrooms and three baths was probably a bit much for a bachelor, but I sometimes entertained and I didn't like using my sleeping room for playing around.

I took two steps in when I realized that something was wrong.

There was a vibration that I'd felt many times before. It wasn't an unpleasant one, not to me anyway, but it also wasn't expected.

There she sat on my beige leather couch, holding a glass

of wine. She had short black hair that was cut with straight lines to frame the high cheek bones on her perfect face. Her ruby red lips barely hinted at the sinister grin that her creased eyes gave away. She wore an outfit that was somehow darker than black, and her legs were crossed, revealing a tall swinging stiletto boot.

She was a succubus.

Not like Serena who just played the part in our past roleplaying fun. This was the genuine article.

One of the magical bits I *did* have was the ability to scan my surroundings. It didn't work in congested areas, but it was perfect for places like my condo. I heightened my senses and reached out to each room, the bathrooms, and the closets. Then I scanned the terrace.

She was alone.

That was good, at least. It was tough enough handling one succubus. Handling two or three would be…awesome.

"Hello," I said after gaining my bearings.

She merely tilted her head in response.

"Come here often?"

A grin.

I took out my phone and checked my schedule. There was nothing on my calendar regarding my having a date today, so this was something beyond that. I thumbed over my personal emails and saw nothing there either. Every now and then I'd meet someone who seemed normal enough but then turned out to be something more. If I had a nickel for every smokin' hot chick I picked up at a bar who turned out to be a succubus, I'd have a jar full of nickels.

So this was an authentic naughty haunting?

Cool.

The question, though, was who sent her? Somebody had to have. Either that or she arrived on her own volition. Maybe she'd heard of me through friends? That was certainly a possibility. I *did* have a reputation in the succubus community.

She was playing it smooth, though. No words, just a batting of eyelashes and a seductively bouncing boot.

Two could play at that game. Not the eyelashes and bouncing boots bit. I mean the part about playing it cool.

"Right. Well, I have to take a quick shower as I have zombie juice all over me, but I'll be out shortly."

She took another sip of her wine.

CHAPTER 16

I stepped from the shower to see that she was already waiting for me in my room, and she was slightly less clothed than before. In fact, the only thing she was still wearing were those boots. She also had a whip, of course. It was a succubus thing.

My horny meter was at full, which was abundantly apparent as I caught a glance of myself in the mirror. I quickly snagged a robe and sought to get the upper hand, so to speak. Regardless of how crazy my libido was, my sense of survival was stronger and an unannounced succubus put me on edge. Hopefully it would turn out to be a happy coincidence, but I had to find out before I allowed myself to fall under her spell.

"So, Gladys," I said playfully, "what brings you to my room?"

Her brow furrowed. "My name is not Gladys."

"Oh right, sorry. Shiela. I meant to say Shiela." I shrugged. "It's been a long night. Still trying to recover, you know."

"It's not Shiela either." She looked almost hurt.

"Kay?

"No."

"Beatrice?"

"Uh uh."

"Hmmm." I stroked my chin and frowned. I had to string her on a little longer. "Well, this is embarrassing. I'm not exactly getting off on the right foot here, am I?"

"No."

I snapped my fingers and pointed at her. "Celia, right? Yeah, that's it!"

"That's *not* it." She had her arms crossed now and she was pouting. "That's not it at all."

If there was any one weak point about a succubus (and an incubus, I'd imagine), it was their inability to handle anything that made their confidence wane. An unconfident succubus was not effective in the least. They preyed on the weak, after all.

"Henrietta?"

"Seriously?" she said with a look of shock. "Do I look like my name would be Henrietta?"

"What's wrong with Henrietta?"

She didn't reply. Instead, she began putting her clothes back on. She was murmuring to herself what sounded like curses. I even heard the name "Henrietta" mumbled a few times, along with a snort.

I had her right where I wanted her.

She was vulnerable.

She was no longer in charge.

"Stop what you're doing," I said seriously.

She gave me an "excuse me" look, raised eyebrow and all.

"You heard me. Stop." I stepped over to her and stared into her eyes. It was a hard stare. The kind of stare that made you uncomfortable. "You came here for a reason, no?"

"The moment is gone," she said with a hint of uncertainty.

"It doesn't have to be." I kept my face taut as I reached out and caressed her cheek, sending hints of energy into her. There was *some* magic that I was really good at. Her mouth opened slightly and her skin began to flush. "Tell me your name."

"Priscilla," she replied breathily.

I removed my hand and walked out to the living room, leaving her behind. There was little doubt that she was standing right where I left her, swimming in a pool of utter confusion. That thought made me smile.

I poured myself a glass of wine and sat in the same spot she'd occupied when I'd first spotted her.

The sun was up and full now so I clicked the remote to bring the shades down, dimming the area perfectly. Having money afforded me with a plethora of niceties, and I did my best to avail myself of most of them.

Priscilla came out a few moments later looking seriously lost.

"Sit here," I commanded, patting the spot next to me.

She complied without a word.

I ran my finger down her exposed leg and her breath caught.

Like I said, I'm good at this.

Just when she was starting to really warm up to things, I pulled my hand away. It was the same game she would have played on me had I not stopped her. Tease and denial were the primary tools used by her kind.

She looked at me with pleading eyes.

"Who sent you?" I asked before casually taking a sip of my wine.

"I don't know," Priscilla replied without delay. "He didn't give his name."

"What did he look like?"

"He was old and frail with reddish cheeks and sunken eyes."

I sat up. "Shitfaced Fred sent you?"

The spell was broken at my outburst.

"Huh?" Priscilla looked around as if trying to sort out where she was. "What's going on?" She was blinking and frowning and starting to look more than a bit irritated. "How are you seducing me? I'm a succubus. You're not supposed to be able to seduce me."

"Do you want to stop playing, then?" I asked genuinely. "No means no, you know?"

"It does?" she said, looking confused. Considering that she was a succubus, it made sense that she wouldn't grasp the concept of mutual consent. "Since when?"

"Since forever. So are you leaving or do you wish to stick around and play by *my* rules?"

"I'll stay," she said. "It'll be interesting." She then pulled back and gave me the once-over. "Wait a second here. Are you an incubus?"

"No," I said, leaning in close and brushing my lips against hers, inflicting her with my spell again. She swooned, which is a word I never thought I'd use. "I'm an amalgamite."

CHAPTER 17

I strolled into the office as the sun was setting. It'd been a fun day and I had a spring in my step. At the same time, I was a bit concerned over the fact that our friendly necromancer had sent me a succubus. She swore she didn't know the reason she'd been sent, and I gave her plenty of encouragement to tell me.

"Lydia, could you please get everyone to the meeting room?" I said as I keyed up my computer and checked for messages. "Something odd has happened."

"You got it, lover."

I sauntered into the meeting room a couple of minutes later. Everyone was looking refreshed and ready for the next volley of zombie fun. I could only hope that Portman's crew felt the same because they were likely to get another call within a few hours. I didn't know that for certain, obviously, but seeing that we were in Vegas, I was playing the odds.

"I know that look," said Rachel, shaking her head.

"Yep," agreed Jasmine.

Felicia merely rolled her eyes while Serena grinned evilly.

Oh, how I missed her. My all-day playmate *was* a lot of fun, but Serena was better.

"So a succubus was at my place when I got home this morning," I announced with a serene smile. It faded quickly and I held up my hands. "Now, before you all start getting any dastardly thoughts about this, I had nothing to do with it."

Rachel looked taken aback. "You had nothing to do with it? You mean you didn't screw her? I'm impressed!"

"I never said that," I replied as if slapped. "I'm not an idiot. I'm just saying that I wasn't the one who called her over." I took a breath. "She was there when I arrived."

"Sorry to say it, Chief," Chuck piped up, "but this isn't exactly surprising. You're pretty well known for your horndoggishness, you know?"

"Thank you," I said, taking that as a compliment. "The thing is that I turned the tables on her and got her talking." That got their attention. "She was sent by our pal, Shitfaced Fred."

"Oh," Rachel said, leaning forward. "Why?"

"I couldn't get it out of her."

"Losing your touch, eh? Did you try all your moves?"

I loved a challenge. "I could give you the full details, if you'd like, Rachel?"

"No, no," said Rachel, waving at me. "We don't need the play-by-play here."

"I wouldn't mind hearing about it," Serena argued.

Lydia chimed in an instant later. "I'm with Serena. Don't spare the details, stallion."

"Unbelievable," Rachel scoffed.

Everyone in this room knew about my abilities, even the guys. The ladies had all experienced it firsthand, back in the day, and the guys had just heard the stories. I used to be embarrassed by my "horndog" title, but over the years I learned to accept who I was. I never treated anyone poorly during my player escapades, unless they were into that sort of thing. I was *always* a gentleman, even when spankings were involved.

"The answer is obvious," said Serena. "The succubus was sent as a test to see how easily manipulated you are."

"That makes sense," Griff agreed with a nod toward Serena. "It would provide the necromancer with a means of understanding your level of self control. That will aid him in planning his next attack. It also poses an interesting puzzle."

I furrowed my brow. "What?"

"Why only you?" Griff then scanned the room. "Was anyone else visited?" They all shook their heads in response. "Then there is either something specific about you, Ian, or our necromancer is planning to test us all at some point."

We sat in silence for a couple of minutes thinking things through. If Shitfaced Fred wanted to get after only me, that was fine, but I didn't think my crew could manage what I'd just accomplished. Dealing with a succubus or an incubus was typically a losing proposition.

"I think it's just about Ian," Felicia stated, breaking the silence. "The zombies never attacked until he showed up."

"That could be," Jasmine said with a slow nod. "They probably keyed in on your signature. You are a one of a kind, after all."

"That's what the ladies tell me."

"Before you go making your ego even bigger," Rachel interjected, "let's not forget that he also attacked Warren and then put a spell against Griff via a virus."

My bubble was sufficiently bursted.

"Hey, Chief," said Turbo as he rushed in with a cart zooming automatically behind him. It contained a bunch of goggles.

"What's this?" I asked.

"They're the zombie trackers you wanted me to work on," he replied excitedly. "They should allow you to pick out the dead from the living with no problem."

I snapped up a pair that had my name on the side and put them over my head. They were a bit heavy and somewhat bulky, but we'd manage. I looked around the room, stopping specifically on Chuck and Serena since they were both vampires. Technically, they were undead, or interlife, as the case may be, but the goggles showed them as alive. Good.

"How do they work?" asked Chuck as he studied the ones he was holding.

Turbo clapped his hands together and took a deep breath.

"There's a piece of software loaded into the connectors in each of your brains. It works via bluetooth, if you can believe it. I thought that was rather ingenious because we usually take a more complicated path. You don't have to worry about pairing them, though. I've already done that. Just make sure you take the set that has your name on it or they won't work." He paused and held up a finger. "Also, I just installed the software a few minutes ago, so if you notice anything weird, let me know."

"Weird?" I said worriedly. "Like what weird?"

"I dunno," he replied with a fast shrug. "If your leg starts kicking uncontrollably or something, I guess."

Chuck nearly choked. "You can do that?"

He paused and glanced in Chuck's direction. "I was joking. Anyway, the goggles only connect when you're wearing them. I'll be able to tweak and update the code realtime, too, in the event that you need changes."

"Ah." Chuck slipped them on and looked around. "I don't suppose you could just make them into sunglasses so they're not so big?"

"Ooooh," replied Turbo while clapping. "Great idea! It'll take about three weeks."

"These will do for now," I commented, "but you *did* make these much more quickly than you'd originally anticipated." It was time to challenge my pixie. "I guess you just don't have the skill to make them lighter without spending a lot of time on it. It's understandable." I sighed. "Don't worry about it, though. I'm sure you'll improve."

Turbo's face grew dark, which was saying something for a pixie. "I'll have them done by first light!"

CHAPTER 18

I hadn't even been at my desk for more than a minute when Lydia called out that we had skeletons pouring out of the graves at Davis Memorial. I groaned and pushed myself back up.

No rest for the weary…or the dead, apparently.

"Skeletons?" I asked as I padded down the steps with the rest of my crew.

"You heard me right, puddin'," Lydia said. "Not zombies this time."

"What's the difference?" I asked, thinking that dead was dead regardless of skin-to-bone ratio.

"No flesh, muscle, or tendons on skeletons, sweetums."

"Oookay." The entire thing seemed like splitting hairs to me. "We're on our way."

Rachel and I hopped into the car and headed out into the night. I was honestly starting to change my tune about wanting more action. Not that kind. I mean the type like fighting ubernaturals and zombies. There was something to be said about having a cushy job now and then.

"Skeletons," I said derisively. "So stupid. I mean, how are they even walking?"

"Seriously?" Rachel said with a laugh. "You don't bother to question why zombies are able to dig themselves up, attack us, fire your gun at you, and even talk, but a walking skeleton has you perplexed?"

I put up my hands in surrender. "Fair enough."

She was right, but so what? There was something about skeletons that just seemed dumb. Zombies I got. They were creepy, stinky, scary looking, and downright gross. Skeletons though? Come on.

"This entire thing is stupid, if you ask me," Rachel whispered. "Some old asshole reanimating corpses and skeletons and doing other stupid shit. Don't people have better things to do with their lives than mess with everyone else all the time?"

She was acting more annoyed than usual.

"Something wrong?" I asked carefully while sitting at a stoplight. She gave me a dull look. "I mean beyond the obvious."

"No."

That was a lie. She was chewing her lip. That was a tell that I'd seen for years.

"Come on, Rachel, spill it."

"I'm fine."

Her trademarked arm-cross betrayed her statement.

"You're obviously not fine," I replied. "I've known you way too long and…" I paused and my jaw dropped open. I'd seen that look before. I'd seen it many times, in fact. "Oh shit. You're jealous."

"What?"

"You're jealous of Priscilla," I said as the realization continued sinking in.

"I am not," she argued, though not very convincingly.

"You have way too high an opinion of yourself, Ian." She snorted. "Ridiculous."

"If you say so," I said, unconvinced.

"What kind of name is Priscilla anyway?"

"Ah ha! I knew it!" Then I realized I was coming off a bit too enthusiastic. While I longed to poke at the wound, I decided to back off. Toning it down, I said, "Sorry. I'm just rarely right in these types of discussions."

"You're still not."

I aimed for a different angle. "It's nothing to be ashamed of, you know. You could easily order up an incubus for hire. I'm sure they'd be just as solid in the sack as I am…in a manner of speaking."

"They're not," she replied and then slapped herself on the forehead.

"Oh, no way," I said, fighting to keep my eyes on the road. She was just feeding the fire at this point. "You've tried?"

"I don't want to talk about it."

"Too late. Who'd you get? Someone from the Incubus Cartel or was it a solo artist?"

"It's really none of your business, Ian," she said sharply. "I'm not discussing this with you."

"Okay, jeez," I replied as if I'd been slapped. "I'm just trying to help."

"How is making fun of me helping again?" I didn't reply. "How would you like it if I started asking you questions about your 'Priscilla?'" She said the name using finger quotes.

"That's actually her name and she really exists," I said with a squint.

"So?"

"So why'd you use air quotes?"

"What are you talking…" She groaned a second later. "Oh. I don't know!"

I didn't want to push her too far, but I couldn't resist. She teased me about things all the time, so a little turnaround seemed like fair play. Therefore, I donned my Ian's-an-asshole-cap and I pushed forward.

"She called me by my nickname, you know."

"You mean 'douchebag?'"

"Ha. Funny." It *was*, actually. "No, I mean the *other* one that you used to call me back when we were allowed to be intimate."

I let the thought stew for a minute without saying a word. She was probably digging through her memories in the hopes of figuring out what I was talking about. The anticipation was killing me.

Finally, she said, "I don't recall using any nickname with you."

The bait was floating before her and she was eyeing it.

"Well, it's been five years so you probably just forgot."

"No, I wouldn't have forgotten something like that."

"It's not a big deal," I said, waving off the point while knowing that my casualness would entice her to bite. "Anyway, back to the skeletons…"

"I would remember if I called you a nickname, Ian," she said with a hint of menace, signaling that the hook had indeed been set. "I remember all of the other names I call you quite well."

"Again, it's not a…"

"What's the nickname you're talking about?"

"Seriously, Rachel, we don't have to go there." Oh, how I so wanted to go there! I was reeling her in now. "Let's just stick to the case."

"Fine," she said and then turned in her chair. "No, it's not fine. I never called you by any damn nicknames while we were having sex."

I fake sighed. "Yes, you did."

"What then?"

"The same one Priscilla used," I replied. "You both said it repeatedly."

"Well?"

We pulled in to the Davis Memorial parking lot and I shut off the car. I then undid my seatbelt and turned to her.

"'God,'" I said matter-of-factly. "As in 'Oh god, oh god, oh god.'"

She punched me in the head.

CHAPTER 19

"Ouch," I said while rubbing my head as we stepped out of the car. Thank goodness her punch wasn't hard enough to make me hit the glass. "That wasn't nice."

"You deserved it," she said, looking like she was fighting to hold back from laughing. "'God?' Please."

"You said that a lot, too," I teased as I walked around the car, but quickly jumped out of striking distance.

We began scanning the area for skeletons. I didn't see anything, so I assumed they were further in on the graveyard.

Before starting to search for them, though, I decided to see if I could spot Shitfaced Fred.

"Everyone, listen up," I called out through the connector, "I know we're here to confront skeletons, but keep an eye out for the wacky necromancer. And let's not leave Warren alone this time."

"Thanks, Chief."

We split up and began a slow comb of the graveyard until we caught sight of rail thin bodies milling around in the moonlight.

Skeletons.

Now, I'd be the first to admit that I wasn't heavily versed in wizardry, but I had my moments. If Fred was in the area he'd probably be connected somehow to the light that he was using to raise the dead. If I was right, nobody'd note it; if I was wrong, I'd never hear the end of it.

"Griff, can you see that light thing Fred uses to raise the dead?"

"One moment." We all stopped. "Yes, I see it."

I took a breath. "Wouldn't the wizard have to keep some kind of connection to it?"

"Not bad, Chief," Warren chimed in, giving me more credit than I'd expected. "Griff, if you…"

"It ends at the hedges to our left," Griff interrupted while pointing. "He may or may not be there, though. It all depends on the level of magic he's using."

I could only hope that he was there. Maybe we could take this bastard out tonight and be done with all of this. My first thought was to just annihilate Fred and stop this trickling zombie apocalypse, but I had the feeling that the Directors would want to get some intel from him.

"Can you guys think of a way to trap him without killing him?"

"Not likely, Chief," Jasmine replied first. "He's pretty powerful."

"I would agree with that assessment," stated Griff.

I nodded as we continued moving forward. "Rachel?"

"Griff and Jasmine are right. We either nuke him or he gets away. I'd vote the former. I've got enough fire to torch the prick thoroughly."

Obviously, she was in favor of attacking at the moment. It probably had something to do with my teasing her in the car. I had that effect on people.

"Warren?"

"I could probably work something up, Chief," he replied, "but it'd take a fair amount of study and preparation."

"No time for that, I'm afraid."

The first of the skeletons noticed my arrival. This was clear because they spun on me as one, just like the zombies had.

"All right, gang," I said while pointing at the suspected location of Fred, "go ahead and nuke the bastard."

The mages unleashed hell at those poor bushes while Felicia, Chuck, and I fired at the skeletons.

They were harder to hit than the zombies because they were literally bone thin. Worse, when we *did* connect, any bone that was struck just flew away. So if you caught a rib, it'd disappear along with a few others, but the rest of the body would stay intact. The problem there was that it didn't impede their movement at all. Blowing away a finger or an arm wasn't going to stop a skeleton.

I adjusted my aim and said, "Target their legs."

That worked, mostly. They were still able to crawl toward us, but they were no longer running. The legless ones anyway.

At first, the skeletons seemed like a much more effective weapon than the zombies because of the complexity of "killing" them. They were hard to take down, requiring multiple bullets in the process. But then one of them made it through and got to me. It put its arms around my neck and just stood there clacking its jaw.

"Uh," I said as the others kept firing at the mass of skeletons. "What's this thing doing?"

"It looks like it's trying to dance with you, Chief," Warren suggested. He then stepped over and pulled the skeleton away and threw it on the ground. "Oh wow, they have no strength at all."

The skeleton went to get up, but Warren stepped on its

chest and reached down, popping its arms and legs from their sockets. He'd done it like it was nothing. It was a bit gross, truth be told.

"Yes!" He did a fist pump. "Finally something I can beat the crap out of." He then turned to Chuck and Felicia and yelled, "Stop firing! I'm going in!"

He rushed into a mass of skeletons.

The three of us stood there with our mouths agape as Warren went completely ballistic. I'd never seen him like this before. He was ripping their limbs away with a maniacal laughter that was borderline insane.

"He's lost his mind," Felicia said.

We all nodded.

"Did you know he was capable of that, Chief?" asked Chuck.

"I really didn't."

In the distance, my three mages were shredding the hedges where the light was attached. The magical mayhem hitting the area was enough to wipe out a band of ogres. They clearly weren't taking any chances, which told me they felt Shitfaced Fred was even more powerful than they'd been letting on.

Seeing that Warren had this situation under control, I decided to run over to help apprehend what was left of the necromancer.

"Stick with him," I commanded Chuck and Felicia. "Just in case."

As I approached the mages, I was getting the feeling that they had done more than enough to kill Fred. The hedge was a wreck, being pummeled with fireballs, ice shards, and energy blasts. It was amazing that it was even partially intact.

"Okay, guys," I yelled over the cacophony of magic, "I think you got him!"

"Can't stop!" Rachel cried back.

"What?"

"Another virus," Griff croaked.

"Oh, shit. What do I do?"

Griff struggled to face me, though his hands were still unleashing streams of power at the hedges. "Knock us out," he grunted through the connector. "Quickly."

"But…"

"Do it."

I jumped behind them and gave three quick chops to their respective necks.

They all collapsed and the magic stopped.

CHAPTER 20

*S*erena was using her healing touch on them after they'd come to. I felt somewhat guilty about hitting them all, but they appeared grateful.

"It was either that or we died," Jasmine noted somberly. She groaned. "This Fred guy is really advanced."

Rachel nodded. "And he's doing this without demon batteries like Reese had."

"Precisely." Griff was rubbing his neck while waiting for Serena to get to him. "The fact is that we are facing a wizard who has learned the intricacies of warfare in a manner we are unaccustomed to. We must tread carefully going forward."

"Thanks for that obvious assessment," I said and then winced. "Sorry, Griff. Anyway, it seems that this time Fred wasn't looking for the skeletons to take us out. He was trying to figure out a way to destroy you three instead."

Rachel looked up. "Why do you think that?" She held up her hand. "I mean, I *know* he was trying to wipe us out, but why do you think the skeletons were nothing but a diversion?"

"Because Warren-the-skeleton-slayer shredded them," I answered soberly while pointing at our resident wizard. "He didn't even use a weapon."

The mages all turned and looked at Warren. He was all smiles.

"I couldn't believe it either," I continued. "It was like watching one of those Kung Fu movies where the little guy kicks the crap out of a bunch of dudes." I had to give Warren his due. He had stepped up and fought like a madman. "You did a great job, Warren. If we're ever faced with an army of skeletons again, you're going to be our go-to guy."

I walked over to the burning hedges to give them a study. The likelihood of there being additional traps left behind by Fred was low, but I didn't want to risk it. I had enough magical capability to be naughty, and it would be embarrassing to die from incessantly firing embers. My crew would surely save me before that eventuality, but it'd take a while since they'd be rolling on the ground in laughter. Just in case, I kept my distance and used my enhanced vision.

Sitting on the opposite side of the hedge was a small box that had a slew of glyphs drawn all over it.

"Warren?" I called out, waving him over. He drew near and I pointed it out to him. "What's that?"

"Rune box," he answered as he started to move toward it.

I grabbed his arm. "Not so fast, Slayer. It could be boobytrapped, right?"

"Oh, yeah," he answered with a surprised look. "I didn't think of that."

You'd think that the one guy who has to study and heavily prepare for doing magic would have enough sense to use caution when faced with something like this. Warren was a man with two speeds: Slow and fast. He either took his time or he knee-jerked.

"If it is a trap of some kind," I said slowly, "would you have any idea as to how it could be disabled?"

"We need someone without magic."

A few minutes later, Chuck stepped out from behind the hedge holding the box. He moved to a clearing so that he and Felicia could work on it while Warren gave them instructions from a distance.

It seemed that Shitfaced Fred was quite the tinkerer. Not only had he instigated a power siphon against my mages, he integrated a bomb in the box that would be triggered by any magic-user who touched the damn thing. And it was more than likely there'd be another explosive connected to just opening it.

I was starting to really dislike our necromancer.

"Carefully unhinge the bottom panel," Warren instructed Chuck while Felicia held on to the main box.

"The bottom?" asked Chuck.

"Yes," Warren replied. "Don't let it fall off. There are probably a couple of connectors holding it. You have to disable the negative side first or it'll go boom."

"And which one is the negative side?" Chuck asked as the bottom gently slipped free.

"It'll have the symbol for negation on it."

"Algebraic or wizard?"

"Huh?"

"The symbol. Are we talking algebra here or is it something specific to wizardry?"

"Oh, good point, Chuck," said Warren. Then, "It's the wizard one. So it's a small circle with two lines coming off it like horns."

"You wizards are so strange," I noted.

Warren smiled genuinely. "Thanks."

"Got it," announced Chuck.

"Okay, that should be it. Just disconnect it completely and

throw it aside."

Chuck did. No boom. Phew.

"Is it safe now?" asked Felicia, looking up at Warren hopefully.

"Yes."

Everyone let out a collective breath of relief. Felicia set the box down as Warren moved over to study it more closely. He was saying "hmmm" and "huh" a lot.

We left Warren to his studies so we could check on our mages.

Serena was still getting them back to normal, but they were looking pretty rough. Between Fred's magical siphon and my karate chop, I'd be surprised if they'd be back to one hundred percent any time soon.

"How are you feeling?" I asked Rachel as I knelt next to her and rubbed her head. "You look like hell."

"Thanks."

"You know what I mean."

She smiled weakly and put her hand on my arm.

That's when we heard a beeping sound.

Faster than any normal could manage, I jumped to my feet and ran to Warren. I cannoned into him while simultaneously pulling the box away and launching it across the compound with all of my might.

It landed with a thud.

Nothing happened.

"Ouch," said Warren while rubbing his shoulder. "What did you do that for, Chief?"

I was confused. That sound had been coming from the box, right? It had to have been.

"That beeping," I said as I helped him back to his feet. "Wasn't that the box?"

"Yeah."

"Oh, good." At least I wasn't losing my mind. "I thought it

was going to blow up."

He gave me a funny look and knelt down to pick up the pieces that were still sitting there.

"Nah, Chief, it was just a..."

And that's when the box exploded with enough force to blow the crap out of anything within five feet of it.

Warren slowly turned to look at me.

"Wow. Thanks, Chief."

"Don't mention it."

CHAPTER 21

"Skeletons?" said Zack as I sat in front of the Directors.

Imagine having to meet with your boss every day to be grilled about stuff you didn't have enough information on. That's what this felt like. I knew a little more, sure, but not enough. Besides, shouldn't *these* guys know more about this than me?

"Yes, sir," I replied. "Skeletons. Honestly not sure why he went with them. Maybe just as a test? They were surprisingly ineffective. In fact, Officer Lloyd had quite a good time knocking them down and ripping their limbs off."

"The wizard?" said Silver.

I nodded. "We couldn't believe it either. I guess he felt like he could finally contribute in some way beyond lengthy spells and diagrams." I then laughed a bit to myself. "Kind of felt bad for Portman and his crew. They were having a hell of a time matching up limbs with bodies."

EQK was the only one who found that humorous.

"Do you have any further information on the necromancer?" O asked.

"The only thing we know is that he's a lot more advanced than we'd originally thought." I adjusted in my seat. "He's been adding spells to his spells."

"Meaning?"

"He's talking about triggers, Silver," explained O.

"Ah, well that clears it up. Thanks, O."

EQK giggled again.

Ever since I'd become chief and had to start reporting to these guys, I'd noticed the tension between them. I guess it was normal for the different factions to be at odds with each other. The pixies were the worst, no matter what the fairy tales said. They antagonized everyone. Turbo was an exception to that rule. He was a decent little dude. EQK, however, fit the douche-stereotype in the supernatural community perfectly. Personally, I loved the way the pixies acted because they were funny as hell, but they were responsible for a lot of angst between the rest of the factions. They were always starting trouble.

"What I'm talking about, Silver," O said with a growl that even Zack could appreciate, "is an embedded spell that gets *triggered* by something else. Typically tampering or magic."

"Something like a landmine?" asked Zack.

"That's the general idea of it," O replied.

"Ah yes," Silver said at length. "I remember those now. Beastly things back in the war."

"Indeed." O had said with a sigh. It was clear that he'd seen these types of tricks before, too. "What exactly has the necromancer been doing, Mr. Dex?"

"Raising the dead, dumbass," replied EQK before I could respond, effectively proving my point about pixies. "Don't you ever pay attention in these meetings?"

"Watch yourself, EQK," Zack said, coming to O's defense.

"Oh, go mark a tree."

I snorted and then coughed to try and cover my mirth.

While I found EQK more my speed amongst the Directors, the rest of them *were* still my bosses.

"Okay, so Shitfaced Fred put in a trigger on the first line to knock Officer Benchley out."

"Who?" asked Silver scooting forward for just a moment.

I frowned. "Officer Benchley, sir."

"No, who is Shitfaced Fred?"

"Oh, uh…" Damn it. "That's what we're calling the necromancer."

"Why?"

"Because he was drunk and…" I trailed off, feeling like an idiot. "Let's just call him Fred."

"Okay."

I caught a glimpse of his face but it disappeared an instant later. I hated that. It's like waking up from a dream that you can't remember, even though it was so vivid you can't believe it wasn't real.

"Anyway, in his last attack he had configured a box that caused my mages to incessantly cast spells, draining them." I recalled the sight of all that firepower flying from their hands. "Fred nearly took out three of my officers with that."

"A box?" said Zack.

"Yes, sir. It was covered in runes."

"Interesting," O said as he tapped the table. "I'm assuming there was a standard explosive attached as well?"

I lifted my eyebrows at that.

"There was. How did you know that?"

"I saw them during the war."

"Yes," agreed Silver.

He had to have been referring to the supernatural war in the early 1900s. I'd read stories about it and heard some firsthand accounts from folks like Serena and Griff. My other officers hadn't been born yet. Apparently it was an all out battle for supremacy in the factions. According to historical records, it was started by the vampires, but they swear to this day that the werewolves had taken the first bite. Many lives were lost during that war, including a lot of normals, and there were some pretty nasty spells, weaponry, and devices built as well. War brought out the deviousness in people, that was for certain.

"Fortunately, I'd gotten rid of the box before it obliterated Officer Lloyd." The Directors said nothing. I didn't know if they didn't care about the wellbeing of my individual officers or if they were all deep in thought regarding the memory of the war. "Anyway, we're still learning what we can about this mage so we can stop him. If you have any information that may help, I'm all ears."

"I'll send details to your mages regarding the boxes I saw during the battles," offered O. "It won't be comprehensive because a lot of the old magic was never understood. But it should at least give them a way to protect themselves."

"You should also have your wizard do research on amulets," suggested Silver. "We had rune necklaces that helped block the effects of those bombs. It wasn't one hundred percent, but it was better than nothing."

"Thank you, sirs," I said, not expecting any additional feedback from the other two.

I was wrong.

Zack piped up and added, "You could also have Officer Logan change into her werewolf form and sniff the area."

"Seriously?" said EQK with a laugh. "You're suggesting bomb-sniffing dogs now?"

"We smell with the best of them."

"No arguing that," EQK agreed, very likely meaning something far different than what Zack had heard.

"Thank you."

"Right," said EQK. "Anyway, the smartest thing you can do is get your pixie tech to create a detection device. Runes, schematics, and bomb-sniffing dogs are all cute, but everyone who *isn't* a complete moron knows that technology is the way to go."

"That's not true," said O.

"Completely false," argued Silver.

"An utter fabrication," growled Zack.

There was a slight pause, followed by EQK saying, "I rest my case."

CHAPTER 22

*A*s soon as I left the meeting with the Directors, Rachel swung by my office to say there was another bit of fun going on.

"Which cemetery?"

"None. They're actually on the old strip."

"Shit."

I took the steps in a single leap and headed for the door. A quick glance back at the offices told me the rest of the agents were already on their way.

"Here," Rachel said, handing me a pair of fancy sunglasses as we got in the car.

"It's the middle of the night."

"Turbo made them," she explained. "They're to replace the bulky zombie spotters he'd built earlier."

I slipped them on and noticed that it didn't darken things at all. If anything it made the night light up a fair bit. How Turbo had managed to do that while still keeping the lenses so darkly tinted was a mystery I'd likely never ask about. I wouldn't understand his answer anyway. It made me wonder what other little goodies he could build for us.

"That pixie is something else," I said while peeling out and getting down the road. "It didn't even take him until morning."

"Yep."

Engineers were an interesting breed. If they told you they could complete something in a week, it'd take a month; if they said it'd take a month—and they were dramatic about it —it'd take a week; and if they were noncommittal, then you'd likely never get it at all.

"How far behind are we on the others?" I asked as we got on the main strip.

"They left just as I was coming to your office. We should be right on them."

I pressed the accelerator a little harder.

"Hey gang," I said through the connector, "let's not engage with the zombies until we're all in place, understand?"

They acknowledged.

None of us had any clue what the necromancer had in store for us, but he'd been getting trickier with each encounter and I saw no point in engaging without first having a plan.

I closed off the broadcast and just spoke to Rachel. "Now that Fred has decided to finally tackle introducing the dead to the living, we're going to have a shit storm on our hands."

"Yep." Rachel was cracking her knuckles. Most people did this as a stress reliever, Rachel did it as a way to signal she was ready for a fight. "I've already tasked Lydia with getting The Spin down here on this one."

That thought made me shudder.

It was quite amazing to me how I could stand toe-to-toe with a werewolf who was hellbent on biting me in two, but I was *not* fond of facing a confrontation against a five-foot-two normal by the name of Paula Rose. She was a spitfire. If she'd been born a dragon, there'd only be one

JOHN P. LOGSDON & CHRISTOPHER P. YOUNG

difference in what she was as a normal…she'd be able to fly.

I gulped.

"I know what you're thinking," said Rachel, "and let me just say…better you than me."

"Yeah."

We parked at the Downtown Grand, where everyone had agreed to meet. It was far enough away from Freemont to give us a quiet entrance. Plus, it gave us time to plan.

We padded over toward the old strip because that's where the reports had come in from. This made sense seeing that it was one of the more populated areas this time of night.

"Obviously we can't just start shooting these things," I pointed out to the crew while checking to make sure Boomy was fully loaded. "Well, I guess we can, but you know what I'm saying."

"What do you suggest, Chief?"

"Not sure, Chuck." I tucked Boomy back into his holster. "Anyone have any ideas?"

"Use our small guns," Felicia started, "get in close, and knock a few rounds into them. Then drag them off. Let The Spin handle damage control. That's their job."

"Ian's afraid of Paula," Rachel pointed out with a nod at me.

Felicia nodded. "Ah, right."

"I am not," I said with a frown. Then I shrugged. "Okay, maybe a little, but that has no bearing on this. We're cops and our job is to protect the people, so we do what we have to do."

I paused and scanned the area to see if I could spot any of the zombies with my new shades. The crowd wasn't too congested tonight but so far I saw nothing.

"Anyone see any of them?"

"Nothing here," said Jasmine. The rest of the crew didn't see anything either. "When we do spot them," she continued, "we could put together a gripping spell and pull them out of the main area."

"A what?"

"It's a solid idea, actually," said Griff, ignoring my question. "We would have to couple it with a sense of compelling, too."

"True," said Jasmine.

"Anyone want to explain to the non-mages what the hell you're talking about?" I asked.

Rachel spun me around. "Think of it like putting handcuffs on a person, except with magic."

"I like it already."

"Freak." She grunted. "Anyway, it's great to lock them down, but it doesn't mean they'll come along and jump in the back of the squad car...metaphorically speaking. To get the person to comply with following you, just tack on that compelling spell and you're all set."

"Ah," I replied with a nod. "I get it. The handcuff one works, but you don't need that second one."

"Why not?" asked Griff.

"They're already interested in ripping me limb from limb, remember?"

"He's got a point there," stated Jasmine.

We kept scanning the area, but nothing turned up. Maybe it was a false report? Just a helpful super who had been on edge lately with all of the activity going on. It'd happened before, back during the werewolf craze before I'd made it to the rank of chief. There'd been so many wolf attacks in my rookie year that people were calling in to report stray poodles and yapping chihuahuas. I think the entire PPD slept for a week when that fiasco finally ended.

"Uh," said Felicia while pointing up. "I think I've found them."

There they were.

Two zombies.

They were riding the damn zip lines!

CHAPTER 23

The zip line allowed people to put on a harness and fly above everyone else on Freemont Street.

I sent Chuck, Griff, and Serena to the launching tower while the rest of us bolted down to the receiving platform. We probably wouldn't arrive in time to meet them at the landing spot, but since it would take a little time for the zombies to get the safety gear off, we could at least meet them on their way out.

"Keep an eye out for Fred," I commanded through the connector, "and don't take any chances with weird magic shit. We already know the guy is doing his best to find our weak spots. Let's not give him anything to work with." That's when I glanced around and the blood drained from my face. "Where's Warren?"

"He stayed back at base," Serena replied through the connector. "He wanted to keep studying those runes that Fred put on that box."

"Okay, good." I sighed heavily and then opened a channel back to base. "Lydia, could you please have Warren work with Turbo on building us some amulets or something to help protect us against these weird wizard bombs?"

"What wizard bombs, honey pie?"

"He should know, babe," I answered, throwing her a little of the Ian charm. "Silver and O had some information about them."

"I just pulled up a few thousand articles on them myself," she replied. "I believe Warren will have his hands full dealing with this, puddin'."

"Well, that's his job. Thanks, Lydia."

We disconnected just as my crew got to the end of the zip line, over by North Main. The zombies were slowly working their way down the steps. If I were in as bad shape as those guys, I'd have taken the elevator.

"Magic ready?" I asked Jasmine and Rachel. They nodded. "Okay, everyone fan out. I'm going to back away so as not to draw their attention yet. I seem to be enough of a compelling spell all by myself."

I moved backward while keeping my eye on the two dead guys who were struggling down the steps. We could have dropped them right there if there weren't other people around. As it was, we needed to be somewhat chilled about this.

Right as I crested the corner of the Golden Gate, I bumped into someone and the word "flashes" went through my mind.

Everything stopped.

Everything.

Sounds, people, cars…nothing was moving.

Suddenly the world went dark and I found myself grabbing for the wall in order to maintain my balance.

At first I thought that maybe Fred had cast a spell on me, but something told me that wasn't it. The word "flashes" was bouncing around in my head. I gripped the wall. No, this didn't come from Fred. It came from that guy I'd talked to at the Three Angry Wives bar a couple weeks back. Gabe. He mentioned that the demon-powered mage we'd fought before was just one in the line of bad things to come. He then said he would be able to help me. After that, he disappeared into the night, but not until after using that word 'flashes' in such a way that it stuck with me. I couldn't explain it, but I *felt* it.

The darkness began to fade and sounds were reintroduced, but they weren't sounds of a lively night in downtown Vegas. They were the sounds of battle.

I was looking through someone else's eyes. I could see what he saw, smell the scent in the air, feel the touch of the rifle he was holding. Even his fear was gripping my brain as if it were my own. Fortunately, I had enough self-awareness to realize that this wasn't me. It wasn't my body. Hell, it wasn't even my era. This was definitely the past. A dreary, lonesome, terrifying past. And it was nowhere near Vegas either. In fact, I had no idea where the hell we were.

As this soldier, whoever he was, crept along, I could see figures clomping around in front of him.

Zombies.

So this vision was a tie-in to my current situation.

The soldier kept moving until he was situated on the top of a small mound. It was covered in bushes, giving him enough cover to do whatever he intended. My hope was that he was just hiding. They weren't looking in his direction and he appeared to be doing everything he could to avoid them.

Nope.

He attached a scope to his rifle and leveled it, scanning the area until his sights settled on his target.

It was Shitfaced Fred. He was younger, sure, but I rarely forgot a face—Directors notwithstanding. If he took out Fred here that would be that. Could that be what this "flashes" thing was all about? Killing a guy in a vision? That would kick ass.

Unfortunately, the soldier didn't fire.

Instead, he moved the scope a little further to the left until he spotted another wizard.

This one was also hunched over, looking like a grim old man who'd had one too many whiskeys. What was it with wizards and booze? You'd think they used it as a power source or something. That thought made me want to grin, but this wasn't the time.

The soldier lowered the scope away from the wizard's head until it was focused in on a small box that was being cradled in the old man's hands. It wasn't one of those exploding type of boxes that we'd seen the other night. This one was silver with black etching. There were runes all over it. I tried to study and commit them to memory, just in case.

The soldier took a calming breath, set himself, and fired.

Everything exploded in a massive flash of bright light as the sounds of screams filled the air.

Present day rushed back in, mixing the screams with the sound of casinos and cars.

I felt drained, as if I'd just been through a real life catastrophic event. I thought for certain I was going to pass out. Plus, I had zero idea of what the hell just happened to me.

It had to have something to do with Gabe, but I couldn't say what.

Still, that box in my vision clung to me. It was definitely important since Fred had been there. I assumed it was his former master who'd been holding it before the nameless soldier blew the shit out of him.

I glanced up and saw that the zombies were only a couple of steps down from where they'd been when I drifted off to la-la land.

That meant no time had passed.

What the hell was going on?

"Everyone back off," Chuck called through the connect. "We've got a problem here. Do not engage with the zombies. I repeat, do *not* engage."

CHAPTER 24

*T*he rest of my crew backed off to give our two zombie pals a wide berth. They were heading back down to where they'd started their little zip line adventure. My guess was they wanted another ride.

"Chuck?" I said through the connector, "what's going on down there?"

"Griff caught one of the dead guys in his gripping spell and it exploded."

"Oh jeez," said Rachel.

I shook my head as we slowly followed the other zombies.

"How bad?"

"The entire area is covered with zombie bits and goop."

"Swell." As if this wasn't bad enough that Fred had turned them loose where the living were, now he was making them explode? What a dick. "Normals took notice, no doubt?"

"Oh yeah. They're covered in it. Most of them are laughing, but there's an old woman down here who is pretty pissed off." He giggled a bit. "Serena told her it was a show."

"Doing Paula's job, Serena?" I said with a grin.

"Somebody has to."

This wasn't going to make my life any easier.

I don't know what, if anything, Fred had against me, but it sure felt like I'd done something to irk the guy. It could also have been someone else on my team, or even one of the Directors. Actually, that was probably the most likely cause of all this, since they looked more his age. Then again, Serena and Griff had to have been around back during the time of my vision. The gun wasn't *that* old.

"Right. How many more of them are there?"

"Three," answered Chuck.

"Plus the two headed back your way," I noted. "Okay, so we've got five exploding zombies."

"And be wary," Griff added. "Don't forget the necromancer."

The memory of the soldier on the field came back vividly, causing me to reach out and grab Rachel's arm for help. She pushed in and held me up while giving me a concerned look. I could only hope that whatever it was that was happening to me would control itself soon. Fighting zombies was hard enough when I wasn't struggling to stay upright.

"I don't think he's here anymore," I replied to Griff with a gasp. "Something happened to me that I need to discuss with you guys. First, though, let's take care of these zombombs."

"Zombombs?" Jasmine snorted with a look over her shoulder.

"That's technically what they are, right?"

"You're so goofy, Chief."

I gave her a tired wink. "Thanks."

As we passed the Four Queens I glanced up to see two more zip liners going overhead. Fortunately, they were members of the living. That was good considering I didn't have another chase in me at the moment.

We kept trailing the zombies.

It was amazing to watch how nobody even bothered to give the dead guys more than a passing glance. To be fair, the majority of people on this section of the strip were normals, so they likely just assumed our zombie pals were actors, drunks, or homeless. Truth was that I'd be hard pressed to argue the point with them considering the way these guys looked and smelled. In Vegas, most of the actors I knew were drunks, and many of them were homeless. It kind of went with the territory.

"Anyone got a containment plan yet?" I asked hopefully.

"How are you set for running, Chief?" Chuck replied with a question of his own.

I wasn't set for it, but sometimes you had to push aside how you felt and do what was best for the team. It'd take a little work to get me back to full strength though. My legs were still a bit wobbly.

"I may need a helping hand from Serena," I said, and then gave Rachel a naughty grin.

"Perv," she whispered off the connector.

"Why?" Serena said. "What happened?"

"Again, I'll explain later. Let's just stay focused on getting these zombies out of here." I shook my head to clear the cobwebs. "But I *am* going to need a boost of energy or something. I'm pretty drained."

The zombies were getting closer and closer to the launch point. If they decided to go up again, that would suck. Again, I wasn't in the running mood.

The area was too crowded to shoot them, though. Time was running out.

I could have Felicia and Jasmine head back down to the landing point and keep tabs on them. This would probably work since I had the feeling Fred just had these guys running on a loop while waiting for me. Of course they could also have been waiting for Fred to leave the area before starting whatever mayhem he had lined up for them.

Again, that memory flashed into my head. What had triggered it? I had walked backwards to keep away from the zombies and I bumped into someone, and...

Fred.

So that's what this "flash" stuff was all about. But shouldn't it have showed me the world from *his* point of view and not from the view of some soldier who was at odds with him? The entire thing was confusing. Plus, it was making my head ache.

Again, I'd have to deal with that later. We had the more pressing issue of zombies on Freemont Street.

Another glance around the crowds in the area told me that this was going to end up being quite a situation if we didn't take care of things. Yes, it was roughly four in the morning and therefore not as crowded as it would be if it had been midnight, but if even one normal figured out what was *really* going on, there'd be mayhem. Not just here, either. It'd go right back to the way it was during the werewolf craze.

I couldn't have that.

"We can't let them back on the zip lines," I said after taking a deep breath, "so tell me your plan, Chuck."

He did.

I groaned.

CHAPTER 25

*W*e had to act fast, which was something I wasn't feeling up to at the moment.

I stopped and moved to the wall, pulling Rachel with me. To anyone who didn't know us it probably looked like we were doing a little hanky-panky, but the truth was that I needed her strength. Hanky-panky sounded good, too, of course, but in my current state of repair I doubt I'd have been much fun.

She looked at me and nodded as Jasmine and Felicia joined her. They were helping to stabilize her, though I'm sure that Jasmine was also funneling energy in as well. Felicia didn't have that particular skill, so she would keep them both on their feet.

I closed my eyes and felt their energy flowing to me.

You'd think it'd be pretty hot to have a couple of hot ladies flowing energy into you…and you'd be right. But it was also troubling because it meant that they were losing it in the process. Still, it had to be done. I needed power fast.

The entire process only took about twenty seconds, but it felt like an hour.

Rachel let go and collapsed into my arms. Jasmine was faring better, but she was a little more pale than before starting the transference.

"Take care of her," I commanded while gently moving Rachel to them. "I have to get this done."

I took off at a full sprint, feeling like I'd just chugged down five energy drinks. There was a potency to mage power that topped those drinks though, and you didn't tend to have the typical crash either. Plus, zero calories. Some of the wealthy hired on mages specifically for this type of daily boost. They'd bring in ten to twenty midlevel practitioners to keep themselves fed throughout the day. I had the money to do this, too, but I typically had more than enough energy as it was. Not after flashes, apparently, but that wasn't standard fare for me.

I could only hope it'd remain that way.

The zombies were just approaching the zip line ride when I came zooming past. The rest of them were milling about, undoubtedly waiting for me.

Chuck, Serena, and Griff had obviously already high-tailed it down the road to set up our trap for these bags of zombie juice.

I slapped one of the corpses on the head as I ran by and yelled, "Hey, fucker!"

That one exploded an instant later, but I was already out of reach of the mess.

Another perk of being an amalgamite. Speed.

I glanced back to see the rest of the zombies were hot on my trail. They were quicker than I'd expected, but I still had to slow down to make sure that I didn't get too far out of their radar. For all I knew, they would stop their pursuit and just head back to the ride and await my return.

I cut right on South 4th Street and spun around to egg them on.

"Here, zombie zombie," I called out in the most annoying voice I could muster.

They were all still coming my way but I slowed up a little more so they could catch up. I didn't want them close enough to start blowing up, though, so I balanced distance and reeling them in until we got to East Carson. That's when I ran diagonally over to the parking lot and waited for them to follow.

My team had cleared out all the normals by setting up temporary null zones. These zones were typically a no-no unless heavy regulations were followed, but the PPD was allowed to use them in emergency situations as long as they didn't last beyond an hour. Essentially, the zones would keep normals away from entering the area. They'd get a "gut feeling" that they shouldn't come near, and it was strong enough to actually work.

All of the zombies had made it across the street except for one straggler. He was hit by a locksmith van. Poor bastard. The locksmith, not the zombie. Chances are the locksmith knew about supernaturals since he or she undoubtedly had to open many doors to many odd places over the years. Still, it'd take him a minute to figure it out, and that meant he was probably shitting himself at the moment with the thought that he'd just decimated a tourist.

"Nail them," I called out, referring to the zombies who were right behind me.

Chuck and Griff began laying waste to the beasties.

Chuck had clearly ignored the point about using his smaller gun because he had his Eagle unleashing hell. I was damn glad they were both excellent shots, too, because it wasn't much fun running directly into the general radius of 50-caliber projectiles and mage blasts.

"No effect," Griff announced as I finally arrived at their position.

"Bullets either."

"Tried legs, knees, hands, hearts, head?"

"Hit all of them, Chief," Chuck said as the zombies kept coming.

I looked around to see what other options we might have on hand. Nothing was really springing forth except possibly throwing a car at them. I was strong, but not *that* strong.

That's when an idea struck.

"Griff," I said while running back toward the zombies, "cast a shield on me."

"What are you…"

"Just do it!"

I was within ten feet of the zombies when I felt the familiar tingling of being shielded. If these bastards wanted to explode around me, at least I'd be protected.

Wrong.

They managed to break through the shield, causing a shriek to jump from Griff's mouth.

Great. Fred had dropped in another fucking trigger. This time it was integrated right in the zombies themselves. That necromancer was really pissing me off now.

But at least it got worse.

The zombies all stuck to me like magnetic mines, linking their arms and squeezing in tight.

I pushed and grunted and even screamed at them, but I couldn't break free.

They exploded.

CHAPTER 26

$\mathcal{H}$ave you ever had one of those days where you just wanted to go back to when you woke up and start again?

There were body parts everywhere, my head was ringing, and my favorite suit was completely saturated with zombie juice. I looked like I'd just climbed out of a vat of slime. It smelled horrible. Fortunately, I had restocked my clothing supply in the back of the Aston Martin. I had no desire to ask the gang back at the office to clean out the car again.

Rachel and Jasmine were approaching on wobbly legs and Felicia was talking with the locksmith, obviously doing her best to assuage his fears.

"Chuck," I called back, "is Griff okay?"

"He's out," Serena replied before Chuck could. "He'll be fine." She looked up at me. "We really have to figure out a way to block these triggers."

"Yeah."

I took off my jacket and used the inside of it to wipe my face and hair. I seriously needed to brush my teeth.

"You okay?" Rachel asked with sleepy eyes.

"Peachy. How about you guys?"

They both nodded tiredly.

"I don't suppose either of you have any gum?"

They didn't.

We got Griff to his feet and started the long trek back to our cars. I took point in walking back since I was dying to get out of this damn suit. A quick glance back told me that my crew had decided to stay out of my smell radius. Nice. The mass of dirty looks I got from tourists was fun, too. I actually *felt* like a zombie at this point.

I didn't even care who saw me change, but my crew had their backs to me anyway while I stripped down, grabbed a towel, wiped off, and then slipped on a clean outfit. I then grabbed some scented spray and coated myself with it, hoping it'd help alleviate some of the stench.

"Smells like you shit a Christmas tree," Rachel noted as I stepped back in their midst.

"Thanks."

"So what happened back there?" Felicia said, clearly ignoring the odor. This was saying something considering her nose could pick up smells nearly as good as it could when she was in werewolf mode. "And I'm not talking about the zombies. Something kicked your ass when we were waiting for those guys to come down from the zip line. What was it?"

Indeed, that was the question. I wasn't really sure myself. It was vivid and more than disturbing.

"After we took care of that mage with the demon batteries…"

"Reese?" Jasmine interrupted.

"Yeah. Well, I went to the pub to dull my memory on the subject and was approached by a guy who said his name was Gabe."

"What kind of bar was this?" Chuck asked with an eyebrow raised.

"Not *that* kind," I replied, grimacing at him. "Anyway, he said that things were going to get worse with these ubernaturals and that he was going to help me."

"And you didn't think that was important enough to share with the rest of us?"

"Rachel," I replied, looking at her, "I didn't even think the guy was sane. I figured he was just some asshole vampire who heard about the latest happenings with Reese and wanted to stick his head into the mix."

We got that from time to time. A supernatural would consider themselves worthy of being in the PPD and go on a vigilante-style warpath. It usually didn't turn out all that well.

"Anyway, he had used the word 'flashes' at one point and I felt something weird at that." I tried to recall the sensation, but it was fleeting. "That word just stuck in my head. I didn't know why until today."

Felicia tilted her head. "And?"

"Since I didn't want to be too close to the zombies when they came down, I backed off. I bumped into someone at that point and the word 'flashes' filled my head."

I recounted the entirety of what I'd seen in my vision, explaining how realistic everything was, who I'd seen, and the details of the runes on the little box.

"Our necromancer was in this vision?" Griff said, still looking a little worse for wear. The question was rhetorical. He was clearly mulling things over. "This is a very rare skill you have, Ian."

"Story of my life," I said, feeling like I was quoting Shitfaced Fred from our first encounter. "I don't recommend anyone seek this particular skill out. There's not a lot of joy in it."

"So the person you bumped into was Fred," Jasmine stated.

"That would be my guess, too," Griff concurred.

Rachel merely nodded.

"Why didn't he kill you right then?" Chuck asked. "I mean, if he's trying to take you out anyway, why not just do it right while you're standing there with your back to him? Seems like the perfect opportunity."

I shrugged. "I guess you'd have to ask him that."

"Not to be an ass or anything," said Rachel, signaling she was about to be an ass, "but you said no time passed, right?"

"Yes."

"So you could have just spun and grabbed Fred, seeing that you'd just bumped into him."

Damn it. She was right. Again, I had the old coot within arm's reach and nothing.

"I am curious why you didn't see this historical flash before," Griff added. "Back at King David's, I mean."

"I never touched him," I replied. "I got close to him and pointed Boomy at his head, but that's it. I never laid a hand on the guy."

We stood stewing in our own thoughts for a few minutes. This was the second time I could have had Fred and I missed him again. I fought to stop myself from falling into a pit of self-pity when Lydia called through with a message that Paula Rose from The Spin wanted to talk to me. I fell the rest of the way.

"Where is she?" I said resignedly.

"Standing by the zip line on Freemont, lover bunny," Lydia replied.

Rachel snorted and said, "Ugh."

"Thanks, Lydia." I turned to the others. "I don't suppose the rest of you want anything to do with this?" They were intently studying their shoes. "Right. Rachel and Serena, you're on the hook, but the rest of you can head back to the office."

"Why me?" said Serena.

"Because you intimidate Paula."

"Then why me?" Rachel asked quickly.

"Because you're my partner," I replied with a glare that meant I wasn't in the mood to play games.

She took in my serious attitude and, in standard Rachel fashion, mocked me by saying, "Phmecause phmour phmy phmartner."

I sighed.

Everyone else had swiftly retreated to their cars and had engines running. I was envious.

"Do some research or whatever the hell you can to figure out what's going on," I called out to them. "I'm getting tired of playing with this damn necromancer!"

CHAPTER 27

I was surprised to find Paula smiling as we approached. This put me on edge because she tended to wear a permanent scowl whenever I was around.

She looked as great as always, dressed to the nines with her standard business outfit, high heels, and body that no normal should possess. Her hair was down, too. That was different. Usually she kept it up librarian-style, which I kind of dug. Now and then she'd braid it, which was great for pulling during naughty time, but that was a subject I couldn't allow my brain to entertain at the moment.

Yes, she looked amazing. Too bad that smile had to be there.

"Hello, Ian," she said with a level of pleasantness that I only recalled from the days when we had started dating. "It looks like you've managed to make a horrible situation for me. Thanks."

That's the sarcasm I was used to.

Rachel stepped up to one side of me and Serena to the other. At least I had a combined front with them having my back. That would undoubtedly put Paula back on her heels.

"I'm gonna look for clues," said Rachel an instant later.

"I'll help you," replied Serena.

I grimaced knowing full well that neither of them were afraid of Paula. They just left me hanging because they knew it made me uncomfortable.

"Thanks," I whispered through the connector. There was no reply, but I could see the upturned lips on their faces. "Just remember that payback is hell, ladies."

I then gave my best disarming smile to Paula and looked her over.

"You look ravishing, Paula."

"I know." And she did know it. She was borderline narcissistic, but she carried it well. "Were you ever planning to tell me about the entire zombie thing or were you just hoping it'd blow by without impacting anyone?"

"Lydia called you down here, right?"

Her eyes went dead. "I know all about the earlier incidents, Ian. Don't try and play coy with me."

I looked around. "Who told you?"

"Me," said Portman, stepping up beside me. "Was I supposed to keep it a secret, Dex?"

"Well, no," I replied, wincing while hoping that Paula wasn't going to go on a rampage. I tried to cover with, "I just didn't see a point in bringing Paula into this seeing that she's been very busy with the…"

"Oh, can your shit," Paula interrupted, her smile fading. I *knew* it was a fake! "If you had told me about this before, I could have spent a little time preparing. Now I have to figure out a way to put a spin on a bunch of dead people exploding all over the place."

"Only two of them," I reminded her. "The rest of them were all wiped out down the street in a parking lot. We were careful about that."

"Was that before or after you allowed one of them to get

smacked by a van, which caused the normal cops to show up?"

"Uh…"

"That's what I thought." What was it with me making women do the hand-on-hip-foot-tap thing? I mean, I think it's kinda hot, but a *genuine* smile would be nice every now and then. "The cops are having a field day with the college kid who got bit, too."

"Bit?" I said seriously. "Someone got bit?"

Portman tapped my shoulder and pointed over at where a couple of college kids were standing around a buddy. There were paramedics with him.

"Son of a bitch." I pushed past Paula and connected to Rachel and Serena. "We've got a problem."

"No," Rachel replied, *"you've* got a problem."

"Cut the attitude, Rachel," I hissed. "A kid has been bitten by one of the zombies." I was feeling grim about what I needed to do next. "Get over here and help me."

I approached the kid as I thought of how best to delicately handle this. I pulled open my jacket, concealing the fact that I was taking out Boomy.

"What are you doing?" said Serena, eyeing me.

"The kid got bit, remember?"

"And you're going to shoot him?"

The memory of Griff's explanation regarding how a zombie bite didn't cause a person to become a zombie flowed back to my forebrain. I really needed to stop watching so many movies.

"No," I said as if shocked. "I was just thinking that there may be more of the damn things around and I wanted to be ready."

It was a lie. She knew it. So did Rachel.

My partner walked over to the nearest cop. "Who is in charge here?" The guy pointed to a lady officer across the way. Rachel thanked him and turned to me. "I'll handle this and you handle that."

"Handle what?"

I spun to see that Paula was standing there, microphone in hand, cameraman at the ready, and a look on her face that said I'd better cooperate.

CHAPTER 28

"*I*'m standing here with Ian Dex, Chief of the Las Vegas Paranormal Police Department," Paula said in her smooth way. "There has been an incident on Freemont Street on the old strip." She turned my way. "Chief Dex, what can you tell us of the situation?"

Aside from seeing Dr. Vernon and spilling my guts about my feelings, being interviewed for the supernatural news was the worst part of being a cop. I'd rather be shot, and I've been shot, so I know what I'm talking about.

The primary reason I despised this part of the job—besides staring into that judging eye of a camera—was that I had to be careful about what I said. Opening up and telling the world about a necromancer being on the loose and corpses crawling out of their graves is not something that tended to go over well with people, supernatural or not. They were used to hearing about vampires biting normals and werewolves defacing suburban lawns, but when you got to the heavier items that impacted *everyone*, things got real. When things got real, our jobs became harder.

127

"We're still investigating the situation," I replied evenly. "There's not much to share at this time."

"Cut," Paula said, dropping her head into her hands. "You know you have to give me more than that."

"What am I supposed to say, Paula?"

I knew she was frustrated with her job, but that honestly wasn't my problem. She was talented, smart, and very hardworking. There were easily fifty companies within Vegas alone that would pay her top dollar for her skills.

"The truth would be nice."

"Do you really think it's a great idea to broadcast that we've got a zombie invasion on our hands?" I asked with a near shriek, regretting it almost immediately.

I heard one of the cops behind me say, "Did he just say that there's a zombie invasion going on?"

"I believe he did," the other replied.

"That's it," said cop number one. "I'm leaving this fucking town. Maybe I'll move to Iowa or something. Nothing ever happens there. I'll be a goddamn meter maid in a quiet little town and forget about all this crap."

"Yeah, because quiet little towns in the middle of nowhere never have any issues," replied cop number two.

"Exactly."

"Have you ever seen *any* horror movies?"

I sniffed at that and turned my attention back to Paula. She wasn't happy and that was just too bad.

"Look," I said, lowering my voice, "you have a job to do and so do I. If you get me to announce zombies on the news right now, you'll be squashing our ability to stop the necromancer who is causing all of this. We don't have the manpower to answer phones, go to every false call that'll come in, *and* take down the bad guys." I let that sink in before adding, "And remember that you'll be making your own life harder in the process, too, because now everyone is going to be *looking* for zombies. Do you really want to have to spin that?"

She scoffed at that argument. "Only supers hear my broadcast."

"You know better than that," I replied evenly. "There are plenty of normals who know about us."

"Name one."

"You."

"Name two."

"No."

She crossed her arms.

"Fine." I threw up my hands. "Cops, bellhops, concierge, dealers, damn near every business owner from the mom and pop level all the way to the top floor of the biggest casinos, the…"

"Okay, okay," she said, rolling her eyes. "I get it. And, yes, I *do* know about all of them. But that's not the point. They don't all watch the supernatural stations, and even if they did they're sworn to secrecy."

I actually laughed out loud at that comment.

The notion of people being able to contain a secret was asinine. Yes, there were a select few who were capable of taking even the darkest knowledge to their grave, but most people couldn't hold a juicy tidbit to themselves if their lives depended on it. The fact was there were already far too many normals in-the-know. Revealing the fact that zombies were riding zip lines and exploding on contact, *and* apparently biting people, was like opening Pandora's Box.

"Paula," I said as gently as I could, recognizing that she wanted *something* out of this, "I can't let you tell anyone about this yet. It's too dangerous." I held up a hand before she could argue. "But we're getting closer to catching this guy. Once we do, I'll get you an exclusive with him."

Her eyes opened wide at that prospect.

"Seriously?"

"You have my word."

That seemed to appease her. In fact, I believe the smile she was wearing now was actually genuine.

And that look in her eye was familiar, too.

"I miss arguing with you," she said mischievously. "You rarely ever win, but when you do it's kind of hot."

I gulped.

She leaned in and added, "I could always braid my hair, if you're game?" She then looked up. "No strings."

"No strings?"

"Rope, certainly," she noted with a wink, "but no strings."

"I, uh… well…"

"I'll be at your place in the morning."

She turned and started walking seductively away. It was one of those walks that made me whimper. Apparently it made cops one and two feel the same way because they were both coughing all of the sudden.

"Okay," I said as Paula departed, "I'll see you in a few hours. But be careful. There was a succubus there this morning and I don't know if she's left yet."

Paula stopped.

"Way to kill the moment, Ian," she said, looking disgustedly over her shoulder.

Then she continued walking without the swaying hips. It was back to that business like strut that said she'd lost interest. I used to see that walk a lot.

"Does that mean you're not coming over?" I called out.

She replied with a single finger held high in the air.

"So…no?"

CHAPTER 29

We'd wrapped up everything on Freemont. Serena had healed the kid under the guise of being a doctor from the other side of town. She had the paramedics put on bandages and such, but she magically cleaned the wound and set it to healing. She then explained to the kid that he wasn't to remove the bandage for a couple of days. It'd heal within the hour, but Serena didn't want him to know that. It'd raise too many questions. The paramedic crew knew the real situation, of course, so they played along nicely.

Portman and his crew would be cleaning up goop for a couple of hours still. I was starting to feel worse for them than I was for myself. Yeah, I was getting coated with zombie juice a lot, but the morgue team had to deal with all these decomposing bodies, grave placements, refilling mounds of dirt, soaping down sidewalks and parking lots, and making sure that the dead were all placed back in their proper burial spots.

That thought gave me pause.

"Portman?" I said just before my two officers and I left the area, "you *are* putting the bodies back in their proper graves, right?"

"What do you mean?"

"Well, let's say that Bessie Maybell Cahill was one of the corpses and…"

"Who?"

"It's just a name I made up as an example."

He pursed his lips. "Why not just use Jane Doe?"

"Huh?"

"I'm just saying there's no point going deep into a backstory for something like this. We don't know any of these people." He looked up thoughtfully for a moment. "I don't think so, anyway."

"Fine," I said, giving up. Creativity just wasn't allowed these days. "So you made sure that Jane Doe was buried in her own grave, right?"

"There is no real Jane Doe, Dex," He replied with a concerned look on his face. Concerned about my intellect, no doubt. Then he chewed his lip for a second. "Actually, I suppose there are plenty of people with that name out there. Kind of rough when you think about it."

"Portman," I said, jolting him from his thoughts, "I'm just asking if you put the people back into the same graves they came out of."

"Oh, no," he replied with a laugh. "That would have been impossible. I mean, I'm sure we got lucky on getting some of them right, but there were way too many bodies, Dex. The logistics would have been an enormous pain in the ass. Just think of what we'd have to do to accomplish that." He began counting on his fingers. "Dental record research, DNA matching, the…"

"I get it, I get it."

He shrugged. "Besides, who's gonna know?"

"Their spirits might," I replied with a hint of accusation,

instantly recognizing that it wasn't the brightest thing to say aloud.

"What?"

"Yeah," said Rachel, "what?"

"Are you trying to say that you're worried about ghosts, Chief?" Serena asked slowly.

They were all looking at me as if I'd lost my mind. Okay, so I was the one who watched a lot of silly horror movies, and many of them had pissed-off ghosts in them. They tormented people, haunted houses and cemeteries, and were just downright freaky.

"Don't look at me like that," I said.

"You mean we shouldn't look at you like we think you're stupid?" Rachel said. "Sorry, but I was never any good at dramatic acting."

"Nice." I took a deep breath. "I don't think there are ghosts either, gang." They clearly didn't believe me. "But if we were having this conversation last week and I mentioned zombies, you'd all be giving me the same looks you're giving me now."

"Fair enough," Rachel said finally, nodding her acquiescence. "I doubt that Fred is going to take that angle, though. It's a totally different tract on necromancy for him. He *might* be good enough to have mastered both, but I kind of doubt it."

"Still…"

"And even if he was going that route, Chief," Serena added, "he wouldn't need an excuse for the ghosts to come out."

"True, but…"

"Dex," Portman interrupted, "I'll make a deal with you. If we suddenly get an influx of ghosts terrorizing the town, we'll dig up the bodies again and stick them in their correct spots. Until then, I'm letting my crew rest up whenever possible."

It was hard to argue the point, so I just nodded, said my goodbyes and headed back to the Aston Martin.

Nobody spoke along the way.

I knew what they were thinking and that was okay. Like I said, the concept of zombies was ridiculous, too. But I had to admit that our seeing ghosts was asinine.

Still, Fred had shown himself to be pretty sneaky so far.

And that was my real concern at the moment.

What did he have planned for us next?

So far he'd spent his time toying with us. It was almost like he had no major plan. He just wanted to torment us—*me* for some reason. But I couldn't buy that because he was adding facets to his creatures. They started out as simple drones, but he'd added more to them each time. Changed their dynamics. And he also attacked my mages through triggers.

The vision I had was the clincher though.

Shitfaced Fred was an apprentice to a necromancer who had once raised a zombie army. He seemed to be heading down that same path. Why he was choosing the methods he did in order to accomplish it, I couldn't say, but there was just too much evidence to think his intentions were anything but dubious.

"Puddin'?" Lydia said as I climbed into the car.

I put my head on the steering wheel, wondering what could possibly be going on now.

Just a few weeks ago Rachel and I were complaining about being in a rut. Careful what you wish for, I suppose.

"Hey, Lydia," I replied tiredly through the connector. "What's up?"

"Are you sitting down?"

I tilted my head to the side and glanced at Rachel.

She shrugged.

"Yes," I said at length.

"I just received a message from The Spin," she replied. "The van was stopped on their way back to the office and everyone inside was knocked out."

My blood ran cold.

"Stopped by whom?" asked Rachel.

"The necromancer," she replied. "He's taken Paula Rose."

CHAPTER 30

Shitfaced Fred was making it personal now.

I didn't know what his game was, but he'd moved from zombies you could kill by shooting them in the head, to requiring that they be shot in the heart, to pointless skeletons, back to exploding zombies, and now kidnapping.

But he didn't just kidnap anyone. He kidnapped my ex, meaning he *was* targeting me.

Then again, maybe I was being too self-involved here. Paula was a TV personality, her disappearance would make for a hell of a story, bringing Fred into the spotlight pretty heavily. Plus, my crew had been targeted too. The mages anyway. But even that could have been in an attempt to weaken me.

Why would he want that, though? Wouldn't it be better for him to stay in the shadows until he had his final attack in place? The thought of him building out some grandiose plan that involved zombies and the city of Vegas made me groan.

Why couldn't he have picked a place like New York or London? They had much larger Paranormal Police

136

Departments there that could more readily handle this type of situation.

But they didn't have me.

Self-involved or not, I couldn't shake the feeling that I was his target.

"There has to be more to this," Serena said calmly as I sped down the street and back to base. "It's obvious he doesn't like you, Ian, but why?"

Rachel turned in her seat and looked at me. "Did you bone his wife?"

"What?" I shot her an irritated glance. "No!" Then I chewed my lip. "I don't think so anyway." The memory of the vision came back. "No, I couldn't have. He's old and while I don't mind a silver fox now and then, I always check them out first to make sure they're single."

"Ew," said Rachel.

Serena laughed. "I'd love to be a fly on the wall at your psych evals."

"Anyway, I'm pretty sure I didn't bone this guy's wife. I'm careful about stuff like that. Adultery isn't my bag." I gripped the wheel tighter. "I even broke up with Paula *because* I didn't want to cheat on her, as you both may recall."

That quieted them. I may have been many things, but cheater wasn't on the list. And these two knew that about me. Yeah, I'm a player, but I don't hurt people…unless we have a safe word established, of course.

"Hey, Chief," came the voice of Turbo to interrupt our silence, "I took the liberty of connecting our cams and a few satellites to the code that I made for spotting the zombies."

"Great, Turbo," I replied without much enthusiasm. "What's that buy us, exactly?"

"I can spot instantly if any dead bodies are walking around. Anywhere we have visual, and with satellites, I can see the entire city and the outlying areas."

"Oh, well that's cool."

I hung a left on to Convention Center Drive and slammed the pedal toward Paradise Road.

"It's *really* cool," Turbo said with so much enthusiasm that it lifted my mood one percentage point. "But there's a problem."

There went that percentage point.

A quick left and a right toward the back of the convention center took us to a major null zone where a hidden tunnel took us underground.

"Isn't there always a problem?"

"Yep."

"Okay, so what is it?"

"Well, I used the satellite tracking system and started scanning the main areas," he was speaking rapidly. "I didn't want to just look everywhere because that wouldn't be very efficient, so I started targeting different cemeteries and I also scanned the major areas of the strip."

Turbo had a knack for dragging things out for an eternity. Where you may say, "I finally got my oil changed," Turbo would say, "The day started with a dark cloud hovering over my rumbling vehicle. The check engine light flickered multiple times, but it never stayed on full. I knew something was amiss so I drove to town, only to get caught in bumper-to-bumper traffic. Time felt like it stopped. People were honking their horns and two men had stepped out of their cars to settle a dispute regarding the right to merge at the last second. The small guy won. The cops showed up and I got to the shop thirty minutes later. They checked every aspect of my car until finally determining that I needed an oil change."

I took a deep breath.

"And what did you find, Turbo?"

"Zombies."

I got out of the car and handed my keys to a tech. He took one whiff of the air and groaned, obviously catching that lovely scent of zombie. I shrugged in response and then cracked open the door to the main building.

"Meet us in the conference room, Turbo," I commanded, preparing myself to wring his neck for wasting my time. "Lydia, please get everyone else there as well."

"They're already in there, honey."

"Great."

We walked in the building and headed directly for the conference room. Turbo was already running around on the table, obviously finding it difficult to contain his excitement. Pixies got excited whether news was good or bad.

Fortunately for him, he wasn't close enough for me to grab him.

The magic users were going through documents that had funny drawings all over them, while Felicia and Chuck looked to be taking inventory of their weapons.

I'd get to all of them in a second. Right now I needed to know what Turbo was all hyped up about.

"All right, Turbo," I said as I took my seat at the head of the table, "enough babbling about. Tell us *precisely* what you found please."

"Zombies," he said again. "I told you that before."

"We already know about the zombies," I replied, blinking. "You built us glasses to spot them, remember? We've found more of the damn things than I can count!"

"Seventy-seven in all," Griff chimed in. "That does not include the skeletons, but it does take into account the ones that exploded."

"I was being rhetorical, Griff, but thanks."

"Ah."

I leveled my stare at Turbo. He quit pacing.

"Can you *please* tell me *exactly* what you've seen?" I asked.

He went to speak, but I creased my eyes menacingly. "And do it clearly and succinctly."

He swallowed hard and looked from face to face. Everyone wore the same grim expression that I was holding. This was not excited-pixie time.

"Right," he said in a hoarse voice. "There is a massive army of zombies heading toward the city."

CHAPTER 31

ot a word was said after I dropped the zombie army bomb on the Directors. They were either shocked, surprised, freaked out, or beside themselves trying to come up with a way to respond…or, in the case of EQK, watching cartoons on the net.

"Sirs?" I ventured finally.

"Has Turbo determined precisely how many of them there are?" asked Zack.

"Just over five hundred."

"You're not going to be able to handle that many," O noted.

"Your powers of deduction never fail to amaze, O," Silver stated.

Here we go again. Whatever these two had against each other must have gone back a ways. My guess was that they were at odds in some war or something.

"I'm growing weary of your remarks, Director Silver."

"Oooh," EQK piped up, "you used his full title. Are you guys going to fight? If so, I'll get some popcorn."

"They're not going to fight," Zack replied before either

JOHN P. LOGSDON & CHRISTOPHER P. YOUNG

Silver or O could say a word. "First off, they're too far away from each other, and secondly we're all in this together. Let's act like it."

I hadn't expected that from the werewolf, to be honest. He was usually bouncing off the rest of the Directors while avoiding taking sides. It was nice to see him step up.

"The fact is that you're right about the zombies," I said as the tension mellowed. "We can't handle this. We can't even handle one fifth of it, and that's because there's more to this incoming army than meets the eye."

"Such as?" asked Silver.

"They've kidnapped Paula Rose, for one."

I thought O was going to fall off his chair at that. "What?"

"He stopped The Spin's van on their way back from Freemont, knocked everyone out, and took Paula."

"But why?"

"My guess is because he knows that she and I used to date." I shrugged because I wasn't certain if that was the reason, or if Fred really even knew about my past with Paula. "I could be wrong about that, but it doesn't matter anyway. The fact is that he's got her and that makes this even tougher to deal with."

"Why?" said EQK. "It's just a wacky normal chick who you're not even banging anymore. She's just fodder now. What's the problem?"

"Don't even bother answering that," Zack said before I could respond. "EQK obviously has issues with understanding the intricacies of human relationships."

"No, I don't," EQK argued. "I watch a lot of nighttime TV about you weirdos. The shows make your handling of relationships very clear. It always goes something like this: A chick sizes up a dude. If she digs him, he gets in her pants; if not, he doesn't. About a year goes by and they get married.

He no longer gets in her pants and she keeps his balls in her purse." He paused. "Did I miss anything?"

Silver actually chuckled at this.

"Right," I said while squinting toward the pixie. This was one of those rare times that I just wasn't in the mood. "Anyway, on top of the fact that her life is in jeopardy, our fun little necromancer has also given the zombies the ability to speak."

"So?" said Zack.

"So they can be instilled with power words," O stated. "It's a means of allowing them to do magic, to a point. Nothing major, but they could conceivably heal each other, launch minor pain spells, add strength and agility, and numerous other annoyances."

Silver grunted. "There's no way a single necromancer could instill all of that power into that many zombies while also playing the size-up game with the Las Vegas PPD."

Something told me to keep my mouth shut about the vision I'd had. Normally I'm pretty open with the Directors, but I couldn't shake the feeling that I had to keep this little tidbit from them. The details, anyway. My gut said that the Directors had to be kept in the dark on this one.

"Maybe he's not alone, sir," I said cryptically, thinking that he may have multiple magic users working with him. I was basing that deduction on my vision. And Silver was right, there *was* a lot of magic being spent here and one person being responsible for all of it was unlikely. "He could have apprentices or accomplices helping him out."

"Yes," O mused. "That *does* seem reasonable."

"Sounds to me like we're going to need to step in here," said Silver.

"We can't make it all the way there in time."

"No, Zack, we can't," agreed Silver. "But we can call on the supernaturals of Las Vegas to get off their butts and help out."

"Now you're talkin'," EQK said with a high level of excitement. "I can get the pixies out there to kick some ass, for sure!"

Silver's shadow turned. "Good. I think. Anyway, unless other members of the council disagree, we'll get you help."

"It's the only thing to do," O stated. "I don't like it, and Mr. Dex will have to be in charge so that things don't get too far out-of-hand…"

"You mean like, say, a zombie-invasion level of out-of-hand?"

"What I mean, Silver, is that whenever we've had to use the people in the past, there have been repercussions." O cleared his throat. "The fact is that we'll be awakening the fighter in a lot of people who should not have it brought to life. Once that happens, it'll make for difficulty in controlling them for a while."

"Okay, that's fair," Silver replied, sighing. "You're right, O."

"Thank you."

"Based on that fact," Silver continued, "I think vampires and werewolves should stay out of this. Fae can manage. Pixies can manage. Mages and wizards can manage. But I would assume Zack would agree that our two people should not taste blood and flesh, regardless if its dead or not."

"I definitely agree."

EQK started doing a slow clap. It was one of those mocking claps that you heard whenever someone said something really dumb, offensive, or just downright douchey. It was a clap that was often implemented whenever EQK spoke.

"Nice, nice, nice," the pixie said in a grandiose voice. "Why is it that whenever *we* point out that vampires and werewolves are huge pains in the ass you get all up in arms?

But whenever we need you to stand by us and fight, you turn around and state that you can't because you'll end up being huge pains in the ass?"

As if sensing another round of verbal lashing was about to ensue, O quickly said, "There are many things that the vampires and werewolves bring to the table that we cannot, EQK. They would be exceedingly powerful at aiding us in crushing this foe, but they are also wise enough to know their limitations."

"Yeah, yeah, yeah."

"Actually, sirs," I said, not believing I was about to suggest what I was about to suggest, "I have a better idea."

CHAPTER 32

The fact was that we didn't need or want a ton of supernaturals pouring out of the woodworks to destroy zombies. We needed a select set who could be trusted to handle themselves properly, stand up to the tide that was rolling in, and be able to get back to being who they were in the first place.

Unfortunately, they didn't exist en mass, and we didn't have time to handpick the ones that could handle things.

And so I decided on a different angle entirely.

"Post-apocalyptic zombie festival goers?" Rachel said, leaving her mouth agape after finishing her question.

"Yep," I replied without delay. "The Directors had suggested that we use vampires and werewolves and pixies and…. Well, you get the idea."

"That would be bad."

"Exactly what I thought." I took out Boomy and sat it on my desk. "But then I had the idea of getting Turbo to enhance a bunch of these Eagles to make it seem like they're nothing but glorified paint guns…"

"You realize this is insane, right?" she interrupted. "What if they shoot at each other?"

Turbo, who was also in the room said, "They couldn't. Well, I mean, they could, but the bullets are full of paint."

"Paint?" Rachel's forehead creased severely. "You've both lost your minds."

"Probably, but tell her why it'll work, Turbo."

"Because the paint contains nanites," he said as if that had explained everything. He clearly recognized it did not because he added, "You know, microscopic machines?"

"I know what a nanite is, Turbo," she said.

"Oh, sorry. It's just that you were looking at me funny and so I thought…"

She snapped her fingers, shutting him up. "What I don't understand is why putting nanites in the paint matters. Can you explain?"

"Ah, right!" His wings started buzzing, which signaled he was rather pleased to be in lecture-mode. "When the paint hits the uniform or whatever, it will immediately seek out flesh. It will then determine if the host is living or not. If it turns out to be alive, it'll leave it alone; if not, it'll shred all the cells, completely eradicating the creature."

I laughed and slapped the desk. "Rachel, it'll turn the damn things to dust!"

The gears in her head appeared to be spinning at full tilt. That meant she wasn't buying the plan. This was worrisome because I'd learned to trust her gut instinct over the years.

"What's the matter?"

She pursed her lips and spoke slowly. "What you're describing would need to go deeper than a simple flesh check. People have cells dying all the time, but that doesn't mean the person is dead."

"Very impressive," said Turbo while clapping his hands so

rapidly that it sounded like maracas being shaken at full speed. "Unfortunately, I can't use the same technology I'm using with the zombie-detector glasses, either. So, even though I'm loathe to do it, I had to bring in Warren on this one."

She sat back and nodded. "You're infusing the pellets with magic."

"Griff and Serena are helping him get everything underway," I pointed out. "Between the three of them, and you, of course, we can build an arsenal of weapons to hand out before dark tomorrow."

One of the many benefits of having a diverse team was found in times like this. Everyone had their role. There was overlap in many areas, certainly, but each of us had a particular skill or skills that the others couldn't quite match. Magic, though, could be funneled, allowing any of the mages to act as a conduit for Warren's spells. It wasn't quite the demon-battery notion that had been employed by Reese, but Warren had explained that it *was* similar to the concept of power words that we feared Fred would employ.

"I'd better get back to it," Turbo announced. "Is there anything else?"

There wasn't.

Rachel sniffed and a thin smile appeared as Turbo zipped from my office. Her eyes were half-closed while she shook her head.

"Only *you* could think of something like this," she said.

"I have my moments."

"Oh, that's definitely true."

It was either a slight or a compliment. Probably both.

"Chief?" Jasmine said, knocking at my door.

"Come on in."

Felicia joined her and they just stood there staring at me. They didn't have to say anything. The looks on their faces said it all.

"Yes," I answered their unasked question, "Lydia has put out a 'Zombie Party' blast to every post-apocalyptic zombie festival goer within the area. Turbo's outfitting them with…"

"Eagles carrying paint pellets infused with magically enhanced nanites that shred zombies on contact," interrupted Jasmine. "We know."

Their dark expressions changed to laughter.

"It's frickin' brilliant," Felicia said.

Rachel's eyes opened wide and she spun around. "Wait, you like this idea?"

"Are you kidding?" answered Felicia. "I *love* this idea. We're going to allow people to have a blast while destroying zombies, and they'll think it's nothing but a game. I think it's fantastic."

I was feeling a hint of pride at their reaction.

Rachel was always pointing out the stupidity of my ideas. It was kind of her job. Not one she was hired for, but one she'd morphed into over our years together. So to have some support from others on the squad made her cynicism a little easier to manage.

"And what if one of the zombies kills a normal?" she asked, attempting to sober our joy.

"Already thought of and planned for," I answered smoothly. This clearly confused her. "You see, *our* job is to make sure that doesn't happen. We'll be allowing people to shoot at the zombies from a distance while we spend our time making sure none of the rotting corpses gets close to the normals."

"Fair enough," she said with a slow nod. "And what if Fred starts casting spells at the normals?"

Shit.

CHAPTER 33

e'd spent the entire night and the next day
building out the plan.

There were eighty-three people signed up to our "zombie bashing party," which started at six. Shooting wouldn't commence until after dark, of course, and Turbo was keeping a keen eye on zombie movement to make sure we'd be ready in time. We had to have all the weapons set, bullets made, and a plan in place to make sure that everyone was certain that this was nothing but make believe.

Having Paula on the team would have been perfect, but she was in the hands of Shitfaced Fred.

My mages had been working with their contacts at the Crimson Focus, and also the Vampire Historical Records Department in order to build some of these amulets that Silver had mentioned to me in the last Director's Meeting. I didn't know what level of protection they would afford us, but I hoped it'd be decent.

Per EQK's recommendation, Turbo built out a bomb detection system. It was keyed to the same glasses that we wore for spotting zombies, so we'd be able to tell in an instant if there were any mines lying around. He'd also had a machine churning out paint pellets by the hundreds. There were already 20 barrels of the things at the ready.

Portman had brought over a fleet of vans to help us carry everything to the site. He needed his team to be there to clean up the carnage anyway, and I promised he could take part in the battle.

Everything was loaded up and ready to go.

"We've got a problem, Chief," said Chuck as he walked up holding a clipboard.

"Why?" I replied irritably.

"Huh?"

"Why do we *always* have a problem? Can't we just do something one time without a hitch?"

"Well," he said, shifting in place, "it's not like it's a *huge* problem or anything. It's just that the mages were only able to put together four amulets for protection."

"That's it?"

"Yeah. They wanted to do more, but…"

"No, sorry," I interrupted, "I mean *that's* the problem?"

"Oh, yeah."

"If that's the biggest issue that rears its ugly head tonight, Chuck, I'll be the happiest man in Vegas."

So we had four amulets and seven officers. I wasn't counting Warren as these were zombies we're going to be fighting, not skeletons. He apparently had a few spells up his sleeve to protect the civilians against magical attacks anyway.

We headed off toward the Tule Springs Fossil Beds on the outskirts of town. The zombie army was on track to overrun the subdivisions in that area within a few hours. I assumed that Fred was smart enough to steer clear of the Clark County Shooting Complex.

"I've been thinking about something," I said to Rachel as we led the way to the event. "You've probably heard that we only have four amulets. I think we need to take them and sneak around behind Fred."

She nodded. "Not a bad idea, actually."

"Thanks." I checked my rear view mirror to make sure everyone was with me. It was pointless because they all knew where they were going, but I was a creature of habit. "You were right about Fred casting spells at the normals. We have to take him out."

"Warren has built up some shielding to help protect them."

"And that will definitely help, but I think we both know that Fred has next-level capabilities."

"True." She drummed her fingers on her knee. "But we can't pull four officers off the front either."

"Agreed. You and I are going to go alone."

"What?"

"There's no other way, Rachel. We have to get behind the lines and take out Fred and whatever other lackeys he's got, liberate Paula, and then lay down fire on the zombies from the rear."

"That's nuts," she said with a laugh. She then followed that up with, "I'm in."

One of the many things I loved about Rachel, and most of my crew, was that they rose up in the face of a challenge. They'd often grumble and complain about it, but they were built for this…literally. The genetic enhancements every PPD officer received made them adrenaline junkies. Skydiving, base jumping, fast cars, hang gliding, and chasing bad guys was a way of life for them. This was less so for the likes of Serena and Griff, but that's because they were both older and more in control of themselves. Warren was also an outlier, unless there were skeletons around, apparently.

"What if he has apprentices with him?" Rachel asked as we continued our trip. "He could also have full wizards or mages, for that matter. Possibly even werewolves, vampires, fae, pixies, and so on."

I winced at the thought of pixies being there. They were as irritating as gnats, and far more powerful.

"Could he really control all of that *and* the zombies?"

"Not easily," she admitted, "but, again, if he's got help from apprentices and other mages, they could be dealing with the beasts."

That was a sobering thought. I had the feeling he'd have a few apprentices along, similar to the vision I'd had back on Freemont, but I didn't take into account him stocking muscle. It made sense. Why would he leave himself unprotected?

A thought struck.

"He won't have higher-level magic users," I declared.

"Why not?"

"They'd be a threat."

She turned to look at me. I glanced over to see that she was surprised at my deduction.

I winked.

"Well done." She said it as though she were impressed. "Mages work together all the time, but our demon-powered pal Reese had no other magic users on staff." She paused. "He *did* want to bring you in on his plans, but he probably figured your magic was too low of a level to be worrisome."

"Yep."

She was about to continue when I held up my finger. I wanted to check in with base to make sure everything was a go. We couldn't have any flub ups right now.

"Lydia," I called out through the connector, "how are we looking?"

"Turbo reports that the zombie army is still en route, love

JOHN P. LOGSDON & CHRISTOPHER P. YOUNG

muffin," she answered. "There are also a bunch of normals gathering at the prescribed party location."

"Thanks, babe."

"Ugh," said Rachel. "Anyway, so he's still bound to have some bodyguards around and even though his apprentices aren't likely to be anywhere near his skill level, it's hard to believe that they'll be weak."

"True." I chewed my lip, trying to think of a way through this. "Any suggestions?"

"We need cover," she stated.

"That'd be great," I said, "but we can't risk the officers."

"Then we bring two solid shooters from the normals," she replied without inflection.

"What?"

"We have two additional amulets that can protect them from Fred and his apprentices."

I gave her a quick look.

She was serious.

"Last I heard, Rachel, those amulets won't stop non-magical attacks." I would have expected a suggestion like this from Felicia, Chuck, or even Warren, but Rachel? No. "Hell, we don't even know if the amulets will stop magic, do we?"

"We tested them pretty thoroughly," she answered. "Doesn't mean that Fred won't have some nasty tricks up his sleeve to bypass them, though."

"Exactly, and…"

"Look, Ian," Rachel said, interrupting me, "the fact is that if these zombies and Fred get through, there are going to be a hell of a lot more casualties than two normals."

She had me there. Fred was heading straight into a mass of communities. People were going to get hurt, killed, and possibly even turned into zombies themselves.

"Uh," I said, my mouth going dry. "I know that zombie

bites don't make living people into zombies. But what if a zombie kills a person and then says one of those power words?"

Rachel groaned.

CHAPTER 34

e arrived at the party point to find a bunch of normals standing around wearing Mad Max style outfits. Ripped leathers, bandanas, dirt smeared on their faces, and all sorts of trinkets. They were clearly into this post apocalyptic stuff.

"They look fun," Rachel said as we got out of the car.

I glanced down at my suit. "I feel a little overdressed."

"A little?" She snorted and gave me a once-over. "You're *always* overdressed, Ian."

The rest of the vehicles poured in, sending up clouds of dust.

Everyone started unloading the barrels as Rachel and I went out to talk to the normals. I had motioned them all to quiet down so that we could give them details on how everything was going to work.

I had to play it cool so as not to give them the full details.

"Hello, everyone," I called out so they could all hear me. "My name is Ian Dex and I'm the Chief of the Las Vegas Paranormal Police Dep…" Rachel hit my arm. "Erm, I mean the Las Vegas Paranormal Party Planning Committee."

They clapped.

"This is a, uh, new committee that is in charge of planning parties for, uh, the paranormal community."

More clapping.

"Idiot," whispered Rachel.

"Anyway," I continued, "we're going to be handing out paint pellet guns to all of you in a few minutes. Then we're going to do some target practice and get everyone set up for the upcoming battle."

I paused and looked around at the nodding heads. Two men in the crowd stood out from the rest.

One was wearing a baseball hat that said, "I bleed red, white, and blue." He had on a pair of jeans and a t-shirt with a pig on the front. The other guy had on a white t-shirt and a jean jacket with the sleeves cut off. It looked like a makeshift vest. They were both squinting with one eye and seemed to be chewing tobacco.

I leaned over to Rachel and said, "I think I've found our two candidates. Back row, far left."

She scanned the area and nodded. "We just have to see if they're good with guns."

"Seriously?" I replied. "Look at them again."

"Okay, fair enough."

"Head back and see if we have any actual Desert Eagles for them."

"What?"

"Paint pellets aren't going to kill bodyguards, Rachel."

She went to say something, but clearly figured out that I was right. With a sigh, she turned and headed off toward the vans.

"Okay," I called out to the crowd again, "in order to make this all official, we're going need everyone to line up over by that little tent there, show your identification, sign waivers, and be checked for additional weaponry. You may *not* use any weapons that we do not provide you."

Everyone rushed to get in line. Everyone, that is, except for the two men I'd picked out of the crowd. They were more of the moseying type.

I stepped over and asked them to follow me, away from the line.

"You two seem a bit out of place here," I said.

"Says the guy wearin' an Armani suit," the man with the cap said.

"It's not Armani," I replied as if slapped. "It's a Kiton, thank you very much."

"And he says we don't fit in."

I took a deep breath and slowly released it. "May I have your names please?"

Baseball cap guy said, "Name's Cletus Coltrain and this here is Merle Williams."

"Nice to meet you both. I'm Ian Dex."

"That's what ya said when you was up there telling everyone what was going on," noted Merle.

"True."

I looked back at the line of people. They were all being processed by my crew, along with the help of Portman's squad. A bunch of others were putting up targets, as well, and it looked like Warren was getting his magical shield underway.

"Anyway," I said, turning back to Merle and Cletus, "you look like a couple of fellows who wouldn't find shooting zombies with paint pellets much of a challenge. Am I right?"

"I like shootin' anything," Cletus replied. "'Cept animals anyway." He spat out a wad of his tobacco. "Ain't fair to the critters."

I was taken aback by that. "Really? I'd have thought certain you were both hunters."

158

"Is this some kind of profiling?" Merle said with a squint that was deeper than his normal squint. "Just cause we's from the south don't mean we's a couple of hicks."

I looked over their outfits again.

"But you said you liked shooting things," I said, pointing to Cletus.

"And I do," he replied, sticking out his chest. "Bottles, beer cans, them little plastic army men toys, and such. Also go out to play in them paintball games now and then."

"Oh…" I felt like an idiot now. "Sorry, I just…"

"Ya thought we was dumb, that's what," Merle stated as fact. "I'll have you know that I got me a PhD in electronics and Cletus here is a research scientist at a prestigious firm."

Again, I looked at their outfits. "Seriously?"

"Yep," Merle said and then turned to Cletus. "Just like I toldya, Cletus, our accents and outfits mark us as dumb. If Einstein had been from Arkansas, we'd still be relying on Newtonian physics for everything."

"Ain't that the truth?"

I had no answer to that. The fact was that I *had* been profiling them. I assumed they were just a couple of gun-toting southerners who wouldn't have any problem popping a bullet into a werewolf, vampire, or whatever else came at them.

"I'm really sorry," I said, and I meant it. I felt like a complete asshole. We all know what Rachel would have called me about now, too…and she'd have been right. "I have no excuse for myself."

"Don't beat yourself up over it," Cletus after a moment. "We get it all the time."

"Well, it was still wrong."

"Yep."

I sighed. "So what brings you guys to Vegas, then?"

Cletus put on a grin so big that his squint drifted away.

He was obviously a man who had some big news. Either that or it was a lifelong dream to come to the land of decadence.

"I won the lottery," he said proudly. "Netted me out fifty million when all was said and done."

"Wow." That was solid money. It was the kind of money that could score you a very nice condo at The Martin. "But I thought you worked as a researcher?"

"I do," he replied. "Well, I should say I *did*. Planning on putting that behind me. The research was gettin' old. Only so much you can do with ants."

"Ants?"

"Yep. Studied 'em for twenty years. Good fun, but kinda grown tired of it."

"I see," I said, though I didn't. Why would anyone study ants? They crawled around, lifted stuff up, carried it home, and they'd bite you if you irritated them. "So you came to Vegas as a treat, then?"

Cletus nodded. "Yep. Came here a month back with my girlfriend, but that 'what happens in Vegas stays in Vegas' thing didn't pan out." He spat again. "She happened along but didn't stay here, is what I'm sayin'. Ended up comin' back home with me. So I left her there this time and invited my old pal Merle for a trip."

"Ain't never been," Merle said. "It's right nice enough, I suppose, but it gets a little borin'. So when we saw about your party, we thought it'd be fun. Could shoot stuff without it bein' critters and without anybody really gettin' hurt."

I was starting to worry that they weren't the right guys for the job. But they had their heads on straight. I didn't want anyone joining Rachel and me who couldn't think for themselves. They needed to be smart in the ways of hunting, which I'd honestly expected these two to be. However, shooting bottles and shooting werewolves wasn't exactly the same thing.

"Gentlemen," I said finally, realizing that time was growing short and I needed to move, "you've proven yourselves worthy of a different mission that will be even more exciting."

"I'm listenin'," said Merle.

I nodded and then laid out the details for them.

CHAPTER 35

*T*wo hours had passed and the sun was starting its evening descent.

Turbo's readings showed that the zombies were about an hour out. He'd upped his count from being roughly five hundred of them to being over seven hundred. Why couldn't it have gone down to two hundred instead?

"Griff," I said as the crew assembled, "you're in charge while Rachel and I are out."

"Understood."

"Our purpose is to keep the normals safe," I explained for the twentieth time. "Each of us swore an oath to that and we're going to keep it."

Nobody replied. Their looks of grim determination were the only responses I needed anyway.

Felicia and Chuck went into gun-checking mode. They had numerous magazines strapped on. These were the kind that were full of paintballs. They weren't the same size as your standard pellet, either. I picked one up and twirled it in my hand. They were about the size of small marbles.

Serena had a table full of bandages, ointments, and elixirs

laid out. Beyond her normal laying of hands, she was also quite versed in alchemic remedies.

Rachel took a moment to align with Griff and Jasmine. Whatever it was they were doing during these little sessions, it got them focused. When they were focused, they were deadly.

Deadly was good right about now.

"Lydia," I said through the connector, "everyone is ready to go."

"Promise me you'll be careful, pumpkin?"

"We all will be, babe," I answered while heading off to my car.

"Dex," Portman called out as he jogged up to me, "I heard about your plan to go directly after the necromancer. I want to join you."

I shook my head at him, which was not something you ever learned to feel comfortable doing to a werebear. Of all the bad ass people I knew, Portman was the only one who could beat me in a hand-to-hand fight.

"I need you to help protect the normals."

"You sure?"

"Yeah, I'm sure." We stood there for a second. "Besides, if we fail, you'll get to meet him face-to-face anyway."

"True." He slapped me on the shoulder. It hurt. "Well, you can't be driving off in the desert in that fancy car. It won't make it over the first bump." He pointed over near the vans where there sat a big jeep. "Take that."

I eyed the vehicle. It wasn't exactly *me*, but he was right that it would be more appropriate for where we were going. Another glance at the jeep and then at my suit made me admit that my choice of garb was getting worse by the minute.

"Why are there no doors on it?" I asked as we walked toward the vehicle. He just looked at me as if I were stupid.

163

When it came to things like this, I apparently was. "Is it at least an automatic transmission?"

It wasn't.

Fifteen minutes later I sat in the passenger side while Rachel took the wheel. She had an uppity grin that even Griff could have appreciated.

So I couldn't drive a stick? So what? I'd never had the need to drive one. My vehicles were meant for comfortable cruising, not four-wheeling. Rachel had explained that driving a manual transmission gave you more control. I had no need or desire to become "one with the vehicle." To me, a car was a machine that you used for getting from point A to point B. That's it. Now, there was no need to have a cheap, crappy car to do that, but that was another matter entirely.

Cletus and Merle were in the backseat looking over their Desert Eagles. I'd made sure they each had two of them just like us. One with paintballs and one with 50 caliber breaker bullets.

"So the real bullets is for any werewolves and such, right?" asked Merle.

"That's correct."

I heard Cletus release a heavy breath. "I'm sorry, mister, but I gotta say somethin' here. Ya *do* realize that I ain't gonna be investin' in nothing?"

"What are you talking about?" I asked, turning back to look at him.

"Just breaking down the logic of this is all," he replied. "Ya broke us off the rest of them folks and gave us a talkin' to, then ya went and found out how I done won a load of cash, and then ya started givin' me and Merle a special mission tellin' us about werewovles and whatnot. I know that junk is all hooey and so does Merle, but we played along." He eyed the real Desert Eagle. "So here we are gettin' special treatment. Can only mean one thing: Ya want money."

To be fair, I could see his point. If I were on the other side of all this, I'd likely be thinking the same thing. It must have seemed rather fantastical to them, after all. Hell, I remember being a kid and thinking that vampires, werewolves, and magic was all a bunch of bullshit. Then I got introduced to it firsthand.

"Rachel," I said flippantly, "would you mind providing a demonstration for our new friends?"

She pulled the truck behind a mound and hopped out. Obviously we didn't want to risk Shitfaced Fred seeing anything.

Merle and Cletus were looking on attentively when she started twisting her hands together. They began to glow.

"What do you think of that?" I said.

"Buddy, you gotta remember what we do for a livin'," said Merle. "This ain't nothin' but basic electronics."

"You might want to hold on," she announced before the truck started lifting off the ground.

"Impressive," Cletus admitted. "Putting hydraulic lifts in is a purdy good effect."

The truck was up about ten feet in the air now. Rachel began spinning it slowly to give us a panoramic view. The lights were off and there was no glowing around the vehicle, so Fred couldn't have spotted us. Plus, we were still too far from him anyway.

"Ain't never seen hydraulics lift this high and do spins," Merle admitted, holding on so tight that his knuckles had turned completely white. "This might be worth investing in."

"No investments needed," I replied. "This isn't a game, gentlemen. Your final piece of proof is about to happen. Cletus, I would sincerely suggest you follow Merle's lead and hold on."

Rachel flicked her wrist and the truck began doing

summersaults. Fortunately, she limited it to three or I would have hurled.

Once the jeep was back on the ground, she cast three small fireballs and blew up rocks around us. Then she cast a small rain shower to cool off our pals.

"How much ya need?" Cletus said with a look of awe. "I'll give ya damn near everything I got. This is gonna make billions."

Rachel sighed, jumped in, and looked back.

"Listen up, boys," she said sternly. "I'm only going to say this once. This is *not* some joke. This is real. I'm a mage, he's an amalgamite, and…"

"A what?"

"He's a mix of a bunch of things," she clarified. It didn't help, but she pressed on. "Anyway, werewolves are real, so are vampires, fae, werebears, pixies, mages, wizards, necromancers, zombies, djinn, shape shifters, dragons, and pretty much everything else you've ever heard of, though most of the other types don't come to the desert except on vacation."

"You ain't shittin', are ya?" Merle said in a shaky voice. His look was deadly serious. "These things really exist?"

"You're about to find out first hand, gentlemen," I answered while Rachel got the truck in gear. "I will warn you that if you don't take this seriously, you'll both end up injured or dead."

We bounced through the dirt, following the route that Turbo had laid out for us.

It wouldn't be long before we were within walking distance, so I reached into my attache and pulled out a pair of black tennis shoes. They'd look ridiculous with my suit, but I hadn't thought to bring anything along for hunting.

"I don't suppose we can back out?"

"Sorry, Merle," I replied with a quick shake of my head.

"We need you guys. If this necromancer makes it through, Vegas is going to be overrun with zombies before the night is over."

"And after that," added Rachel, "it's only a matter of time before they branch out to other cities."

"Well, shit," Cletus said and then spit a wad of tobacco out the back, making me suddenly glad that the jeep had no doors or top. "Shoulda just stayed home with Vera."

"Yep," agreed Merle.

CHAPTER 36

We arrived at the stopping point and jumped out. Everyone had their amulets on and weapons at the ready.

I had no idea what to expect from Shitfaced Fred. My guess was that he wouldn't be stupid enough to bypass covering his back. There were bound to be sentries, bodyguards, and notification runes. Hopefully those runes weren't tied to explosives, but Turbo's adjustment to our glasses would allow us to spot those pretty easily.

"It's go time," I said as I started up the small hill that separated us from Fred and his army. "Keep your wits about you. There's bound to be trouble soon."

"Chief," Chuck called through the connector, "we've made contact. The zombies are flowing in and the normals are lighting them up."

"Great. Keep us posted."

I heard yelling in the distance. It sounded like someone was pretty pissed off. That had to be Fred or one of his lackeys.

"We just tripped a notification rune," Rachel said.

"How do you know?"

"Felt it."

"I thought you needed some type of spell for spotting those."

"You do," she replied. "I didn't spot it. I tripped it. I don't need a spell to know if I set off one of them."

In support of Rachel's statement, a couple of creatures appeared at the top of the hill in front of us. I zoomed in and saw two werewolves eying us. There was drool dripping from their mouths. Great. Hungry werewolves.

"What's them things?" Merle asked.

"I think you know," I answered while taking out Boomy. I kept Boomy Jr.—which is what I named the Desert Eagle that was built to use paintballs—tucked away. It wouldn't do any good against naughty doggies. "Take out your real guns and get ready to shoot." I stopped and glanced back. "Only fire if they get past me."

"But they ain't even movin' after us," Cletus said. The werewolves began slinking our way. "Okay, maybe they is."

"Just keep cool and aim carefully," I said in a calm voice. "We do this all the time. You'll be fine."

Rachel's hands lit up and she got ready to launch fireballs at the beasties, but I pushed her hands down. She groaned. Our agreement was that she wouldn't use up her magic until we were facing other magic users. We didn't have backup on the mage front, after all.

"Watch them," I commanded as I moved forward to intercept the wolves.

Once we got within one hundred yards of each other, they broke into a run.

I set myself and slowed my breathing, taking aim at the one on my left. He dropped an instant later. The one on the right followed shortly thereafter.

"Damn, son," said Cletus, stepping up next to me. "That

was some mighty fine shootin' there. I'd hate to see what you could do to a beer can!"

"Thanks."

We kept moving forward into the darkness. There was a hint of a glow not too far ahead, which had to be where Fred and his crew were strolling along behind the action.

We stopped and looked at the wolves I'd just wasted. They'd gone back to their normal bodies, except for chunks that were missing due to our 50-caliber rounds. I checked them over to see if they had any way to communicate. A crackling sound came through from near the larger of the two. Rachel reached down and picked it up, handing it to me.

It looked like a small speaker with a button on the side.

The thing crackled again and I heard someone say, "Status?"

I looked at the others and shrugged.

"All clear," I replied in a growl after pressing the little button.

We waited.

"Good," the response came finally. "Keep your eyes open."

This time, I didn't answer. I had no protocol and didn't know their rules, so I wasn't about to take a chance and screw up. It had already been a risk to reply at all, but I figured that if it worked, we wouldn't have another ten of the things coming to check us out.

"Why'd ya growl?" asked Merle.

"So they'd think I was a werewolf."

"Ah yeah, s'pose that makes sense."

We cleared the next hill and looked down over a large expanse. I'd been right about the glow. It was definitely coming from Fred's advancing group.

Another zoom showed me a mass of zombies leading the way. A small group of slouched people were behind them. These had to be the necromancer apprentices. At least if you based them on the description that O had given me. Further back there were a number of zombies mixed in with wolves, vampires, and a succubus.

"Priscilla?" said Rachel as she cracked her neck from side-to-side.

"Hard to say from here," I replied, though it did look like her. "She was a nice girl, though, Rachel. No reason to get all medieval on her."

Rachel turned slowly toward me. "She's a succubus, idiot. There's no such thing as a nice succubus."

"Stereotyping is wrong."

"Ya got that right," Cletus said. "And Mr. Dex here oughta know since he done did it to us just a couple hours back."

You just couldn't win with some folks.

We kept up our pace, until we were within range of doing some damage. I was glad we'd brought along the two normals because we were going to need some firepower against all of these bodyguards. Turning to look at Cletus and Merle, I could only hope they were up for it.

Just in case, I stopped and motioned everyone to hunker down.

"Are you two going to be okay here?" I asked Cletus and Merle, recalling how they were only into shooting beer cans and bottles. "What we're going up against are living creatures. Now, they're bent on killing you, me, and everyone they can get their hands on...but they're still alive."

"From what you said before, we ain't got much of a choice," Merle replied, looking less than okay. "Besides, it's not like I'm shooting some defenseless deer who just stopped off at the pond for a quick sip."

"You're really not," I agreed. "These things will rip you to pieces. And if they get past us, they'll head to Vegas and tear apart everyone else, too."

"Then I guess we gotta do what we gotta do," Merle said,

clearly trying to harden his resolve, though he still looked very uneasy.

It was more than unfair to throw these two into this situation, but we needed them. Vegas needed them.

"Cletus," I said, "are you ready for this?"

"I'll be fine." Cletus seemed to be handling this a little better than his pal. He must have sensed that I'd noticed that, because he added, "Fact is that we gotta get to work. How many times is we gonna be able to put up a fight against stuff like this? They get past us and this town is done for. Where I'm from, we don't back down in the face of wrongdoing. Merle and me'll stand up and fight, mister. Ain't that right, Merle?"

"Damn straight, Cletus," Merle replied, his face creasing back into that squint he'd had when we first met. Obviously Cletus had played the right chord. He grabbed a fresh wad of chew and stuck it into his mouth. "Sittin' around jawing about it ain't gettin' us nowhere. Let's open us a can of whoopass on these suckers."

CHAPTER 37

$\mathcal{R}$achel hung back so she could keep a wide view on things. The hope was that she'd be able to knock out anything that got too close to Cletus and Merle. The second hope was that these amulets would afford us enough protection against anything Fred and his pals might throw our way.

"Remember," I whispered as we continued moving, "left hand is the paintball gun. That's for zombies. Right hand contains the breaker bullets that are for the rest of them. We can all be shot with the paintballs and it won't do anything but sting a little because of the enhancements made by Turbo, but the breakers will kill us. Clear?"

They replied by giving a sinister nod.

It was good to see they were ready for action.

Then Merle said, "How can you tell the difference between a zombie and the others?"

I pointed at a zombie. Its gait was staggered, like a drunkard who needed to sleep it off. Not unlike the image of Fred when he'd fooled us back by King David's. I grunted at the thought.

JOHN P. LOGSDON & CHRISTOPHER P. YOUNG

"Got it," Merle stated.

"Let's stick together," I added as I lifted up Boomy and took aim at the nearest vampire's back. "Nobody runs off."

In response, Merle had his paint gun aimed at the zombie I'd pointed at while aiming his standard Eagle at a werewolf. Cletus had taken on a similar stance.

Not to be outdone, I withdrew Boomy Jr. and had both at the ready.

"Hold steady until I give the word," I commanded and then called back to Chuck through the connector. "What's the status, Chuck?"

"We're getting swarmed here," he replied through ragged breaths. "There are paint pellets zipping all over the place, and they're working like a charm, but there's just too many of them. We're struggling, Chief."

"Understood. We're about to engage from the rear, so I have a feeling you're about to get a slight reprieve."

"Could use it."

"Roger that," I agreed. "Hang tight."

I gave Merle and Cletus one last glance. They clearly had gotten over their nerves because those guns were barely shaking, and they'd been holding them a while. I guess Cletus's speech had really struck a nerve with Merle.

"On three, gentlemen," I announced. "One…two…three!"

We all pulled our triggers and the battle was on.

Bodies dropped, howls rang out, and zombies turned to dust. Those paint pellets were incredible, and they had to be because we had awakened the bodyguards while letting Fred know that we had arrived.

The beasts spun around and started their counterassault.

They were flying in at speeds that were bound to be too much for the likes of Cletus and Merle. Fortunately, Rachel was there to send fireballs into the mix. I sure as hell was glad that these amulets were shielding off any heat that got too close. We'd have been toast otherwise.

"Just keep firing," I called out as the screams increased from the oncoming rush of beasts. "Don't let up even for a second."

"Gotta change ammo at some point," Cletus yelled back.

"Well, yeah, obviously, but just be quick about it."

A lightning bolt zigzagged its way through the oncoming bodies, striking my shield and dissipating. That solidified the fact that Fred knew we were here. Another bolt came from the sky in a huge arc that slammed into the ground nearby, throwing us from our feet. Obviously he had ways of impeding our progress without directly hitting us. It slowed up his own followers too, though.

"Ian," Rachel called out.

I spun around to see two zombies were damn near on her, and she was already having words with a vampire.

Just as I was raising my gun, Merle turned those two zombies to dust and Cletus took out the chick that Rachel had been wrestling with.

Impressive.

Not time for kudos, though. We had to keep fighting or we'd end up as part of Shitfaced Fred's army. I didn't have any interest in volunteering at this stage of my life, and I certainly didn't want to *be* volunteered in the afterlife.

"There's a brief turn here, Chief," Chuck called through the connector. "You're attacking?"

"I wouldn't say that," I replied after dropping a fae. "We started it, but it's been all defense since then."

"Well, you've done something right because we've been able to take them out in double time."

"Good, glad to have helped."

The word "helped" was said with a grunt as a vampire cannoned into me after being shot by Merle. I rolled back to my feet just in time to get knocked on my ass again by a damn lightning bolt.

"Rachel," I said calmly, after expertly swapping in fresh magazines, "I'm tiring of this. We need to break through."

"It'll cost energy."

"I think it already is," I replied. "Do it or I'm going to have to jump into Freeze again."

"Okay, but…"

"Wait," I said, scanning the area. "Scratch that. I've got a better idea."

"Haste?"

"Yep."

"Shit," she said. "All right. Tell Cletus and Merle to cover their eyes when I yell, and to be ready to run back to me. I'm going to flash the area to give you time."

I told them.

Ten seconds later, Rachel yelled "Now" and a light hit with such power that it nearly blinded me *through* my shut eyes.

Creatures groaned and screamed and fell to the ground, writhing in pain. The zombies were still moving, clearly not caring about their eyesight. Cletus and Merle were taking care of them decently, though they were complaining about seeing spots.

It was time for me to move.

Fast.

Very fast.

CHAPTER 38

My eyes were already closed, but I moved into a state of instant calm. I had to shut out everything that was going on in the world in order to activate Haste.

Screams became distant hums, magical blasts were nothing but a dull breeze…

Silence.

Deadness.

I'd hit my core.

I had a number of resources at my disposal, depending on the situation. There were a few that I knew about, but they had been discovered over time, meaning there were likely more yet to be uncovered. I knew I could freeze my emotions, go into a berserker mode that leveraged fear, summon strength, haze my physical presence, preserve oxygen, and go into a level of speed and accuracy that would make me a blur.

I named the last one on the list "haste." I wasn't exactly creative about naming these things.

There were many methods to calling up these skills, but

most of them required that I go into a trance-like state for a few moments. This made me vulnerable, which is why Rachel covered me like she did.

I called upon Haste.

My body began to tremble as the rush of noise came back.

There was a vampire standing above me with his fist pulled back. He was preparing to knock me into yesterday when a breaker ripped through his chest and threw him backwards. Even though this had happened in an instant, to me it was like watching the scene unfold in slow motion.

Haste was in effect.

I jumped to my feet and scanned the area.

Bodies were moving at fifty-percent their normal speed from my perspective, which meant they would see me as having a major spring in my step.

Rachel had her blade out and was in the process of gutting Priscilla. It was disturbing enough to watch her do something like that at full-speed. In slow motion, it was enough to make me gag. And dammit, I'd just boned that succubus. The smirk on Rachel's face read "mission complete."

Cletus and Merle fired off their weapons like seasoned cops. It seems they just needed to get past their fear.

A hand landed on my shoulder.

I spun and placed Boomy against the chest of a vampire that I could have sworn I ended before going into Haste. The breaker tore through her chest and blew a hole out her back. I fired two more for good measure. Obviously she'd somehow survived my first encounter with her, so I wanted to be sure she wouldn't come back from this one.

A voice called with a long, drawn out word. It belonged to a fae who was pointing at a fallen werewolf about ten feet from me. At first I thought maybe she wanted the doggie to stop what it was doing and stand on her left, but then I realized she was using a power word to bring the thing back to life. In other words, she'd said "heal," not "heel."

We couldn't have her continuing her doctoring ways.

I brought Boomy up and placed a breaker right through the fae's neck, cutting off her ability to speak along with her ability to live. Another breaker interrupted the werewolf's healing phase. He was out.

Seeing that it was tough enough to beat these damn things without healers, I turned my focus on eradicating them.

There were three within the area, aside from the fae I'd already dealt with.

I ran at full speed toward the nearest one.

It was a werewolf who had not fully transitioned from its normal mode. I placed a breaker bullet right in his chest as I leapt in the air, clearing his body as he flew backwards from the impact.

A mage, who had seemingly managed to deal with our speed differential, fired an energy beam at me, but my amulet warded it off. She looked confused by this, and that gave me time to put a bullet between her eyes. It bounced off whatever shielding she had in place.

It seemed we were at a standstill.

Unfortunately for her, I wasn't limited to using Boomy.

I bolted at her as she fumbled to cast another spell. A basic fireball launched in my direction two seconds before I tackled her. She gasped for breath, making it clear that I'd knocked the wind out of her.

"Sorry, sister," I said as I put Boomy to her head and ended her anxiety.

A werebear that I'd somehow missed—which was not an easy thing to do—lifted me up and launched me a good ten feet away. Either he was modified or his adrenaline had bumped him up to my speed because he was on me faster than I could pull up Boomy.

"Oh damn," I said as a massive paw knocked the hell out of me.

He was swinging for the fences and I had no way to stop him other than using my arms to protect myself as much as possible.

The ferociousness of his swipes were wearing me out fast.

I had to think of something.

He gave me the opportunity when he reared up and roared so loudly that I thought I was going to shit myself.

Some people sought honorable ways to battle. They would just as soon die instead of resorting to something deemed questionable. Me, I didn't give a damn if my methods were naughty. My goal was to stay alive when I was facing a bad guy. Anything beyond that, didn't matter to me one bit.

And so I snaked out a hand, gripped the werebear by his balls and said, "Stop!"

He froze in place, realizing the gravity of the situation.

"Okay, pal," he said with a gulp. "Whatever you say. Just keep the jewels in place, yeah?"

"How are you moving so fast?"

"Wizard cast some speed spell on me," he answered. "Said you were moving faster than you should be and wanted to even the playing field."

"Why are you supporting this wizard?"

"Ten bucks is ten bucks, pal." He swallowed hard. I twisted his sack slightly. "Okay, okay! The truth is that he's my brother-in-law. My wife's been riding me to help him out with this venture. Things haven't exactly been great at home."

"Oh," I said, relaxing my grip slightly. "Sorry."

"Honestly," he said between short breaths, "you gripping my tenderviddles is about the most action I've had in a year."

"Ew." I gave him a sour look, but I wasn't about to release him just yet. If I did, he'd just redouble his efforts. There's no way he'd give me another chance to get free. "So you're doing this for marital reasons?"

"And the money," he admitted. "Both."

"You realize we're going to kill you, though, right?"

"Only if I don't kill you first," he argued. I twisted again. "Ahhh! Right! I get your point."

"What about the rest of these people? Are they in a similar situation?"

"No, no," he answered with a grunt. "Just me. Aren't many werebears in town, you know."

"I only knew of one, until now."

"Me, too."

I looked at him funnily. "Who?"

"Rick Portman. Works at the morgue. We're drinking buddies."

"Portman is with me."

"Oh yeah?" He tried to smile, but my grip on his nethers made it look more like he had gas. "Never mentioned it."

"What's your name?" I said as I reached down with my other hand to pick up Boomy.

"Harvey Smith," he answered.

"Okay, Harvey," I said, feeling bad about having to kill Portman's pal, "Have you killed anyone for these wizards yet?"

"No," he answered seriously. "I wasn't planning to kill you either, until you grabbed my nuts anyway. Was told to knock you out and bring you back to the boss."

"Seriously?"

"Yeah," he said. "None of you are supposed to be killed."

"Interesting."

181

I pointed Boomy to the left and placed a breaker bullet in the chest of a vampire that had been slowly sneaking up on us. He was still in go-slow mode, after all.

Then I placed Boomy on Harvey's chest and let go of his balls. He breathed heavily.

"How do you feel about your brother-in-law?"

Harvey was wincing. "Hate him nearly as much as I hate his sister."

"Good."

"Good?"

"Yeah," I said. "You're working for us now."

"I am?"

I pressed Boomy against his chest a little harder. "Unless you'd rather die?"

"Always wanted to help the Paranormal Police Department," he said with a gulp.

CHAPTER 39

*T*made sure that Rachel and the crew knew not to
fire at Harvey.

There was something to be said about having a werebear
on your side in general, but one who could move with the
same speed I was able to was priceless.

Harvey and I were cutting a swath right though the
bodyguards like they were nothing. I was using my guns and
Harvey was just ripping them to shreds. But those power
word yelling bastards kept healing them.

Harvey charged a vampire "healer" and made quick work
of him.

The second one was standing on a ledge above the fray
with his little purple outfit and green hat.

It was a damn pixie and he was bouncing around full
speed like me and Harvey.

I ran around the hill and ran up to him from behind, just
as he was about to use his little wand to send a charge of
something at Harvey. Obviously he'd spotted that the
werebear had changed sides. And now that Harvey was on
my side, it was my job to protect him as best I could.

183

"Nope," I said, plucking the wand from the pixie's hand.

He spun around and looked cross. "Give me that back, you dick fume."

"Dick fume?" I said. "I've been called a lot of things, but that's a first."

"Do I look like I care?" he retaliated, crossing his arms. Then his eyes grew wide, his expression changed to one of surprise, he pointed, and yelled, "Look out!"

Instead of turning, I merely ducked.

It was a ruse.

He started to fly using his little pixie wings.

Not on my watch.

I snapped him from the air and brought him to eye level, giving him a devilish glare. Now, it must be said that your average pixie is not easily intimidated. It's like how a chihuahua is more than willing to go toe-to-toe with a great dane. It's not that they have even the slightest chance of winning that battle, but the chihuahua doesn't know this until it's too late. And, to be fair, the great dane second-guesses things because that damn chihuahua is far more confident about the outcome of things than he should be.

Fortunately, I knew pixies pretty well. They were masters at thievery, sneak attacks, and being assholes.

"Where do you think you're going?" I said powerfully.

"Your mom's house."

I blinked at him. "What?"

"I heard she was lonely. Figured I could slip her a little pixie-lovin'."

"Very little," I countered.

He frowned. "I'm above average for my size, I'll have you know."

"Oh, my apologies, then," I said mockingly. "That would make you still way too little for my mom."

"She gets around, eh?"

There was little point trying to get the upper hand against a pixie in a battle of insults. They were just too good at it. It was their primary skillset, after all. Yes, they did magic, too, but mostly they were great at annoying people into submission. If you weren't careful, they'd divert your attention and then attack.

"I don't have time for this," I said and then launched the pixie with a full throw at Harvey.

The pixie yelled "Priiiiiiick" back at me while giving me the finger. A split-second later he'd become a snack for Harvey the werebear.

"Chief," Chuck said through the connector as I felt Haste starting to slow, "we've got things under control here except for the power word guys. They're a pain!"

"We've just destroyed ours," I replied. "I've turned one of the bad guys to our side, too."

"How did you manage that?" asked Griff.

"Made him an offer he couldn't refuse," I replied. "You have to take out those healers, Griff. If you don't, we're done for."

"We're working on it. Are you making any progress toward stopping the wizard?"

"Just about to head into his circle," I replied after shearing off half the head of a fae with Boomy. "Our new pal is going to deliver us as prisoners."

"What?" said Rachel before Griff could reply.

"All part of my plan."

"You planned for this?" She grunted. "I don't remember hearing about this part of the plan. I would have remembered it, too, because it's crazy."

I ducked under a swing from a werewolf and kicked out at his knee, cracking it and sending him to the ground howling. A nicely placed bullet ended his anguish.

"I know it's crazy," I said, "which is why it'll work. I

thought we'd be able to do a straight assault, but we're already wearing out and Haste is about gone."

And it was. I was slowing back to normal speed.

The beasties were all but decimated by the time I made my final lap. Haste was done. This sucked because I was now exhausted. One of the rough parts about using my special skills was how wiped out I became when I was done.

But this time I was prepared.

Knowing that I was likely to drop into these modes, I had Serena whip me up a batch of replenishing energy. She used to do this during our sexcapades back in the day. Yes, there was a time when we could quite literally play "Bad cop, naughty cop" all weekend long.

I downed the elixir and my energy came back to full within seconds.

Eventually, I'd pay the price. You couldn't borrow energy without it catching up to you. Once this was said and done, I'd have to sleep for a few days. That assumed we got through this in one piece. If not, I'd sleep a lot longer.

Cletus wasted the last of the zombies while Merle dropped the final vampire.

Everyone was exhausted but me. I had six vials of the stuff left, though, so I handed one to Rachel, two to Harvey, and one to Cletus and Merle to share. Hooking up normals with this stuff was dicey, so I wanted to make sure they didn't get a full shot.

"Now that everyone is back to one hundred percent," I said, "it's time to pay a visit to Fred."

CHAPTER 40

"Who is Fred?" Harvey asked after introductions.

"Your brother-in-law," I replied. "He's been a real pain in the ass over the last few days and it looks like he wants be even naughtier."

"My brother-in-law's name is Chip," Harvey corrected. "I don't know anyone named Fred." He looked up suddenly. "You sure you got the right fight, pal?"

"I didn't know his actual name, and I wasn't going to go around calling him 'old guy' all the time."

"Chip's not old. He's about my age." Then he snapped his fingers. "Wait, you're talking about Chip's boss, right?"

"I guess so," I answered. "You'd said that the boss wanted us brought in alive, so I assumed that your brother-in-law was the boss."

"Nah. Chip's a mid-level mage."

"But you said the boss wanted us brought back alive, right?"

"Yep, and I said that because Chip said that. I was just regurgitating."

Rachel stuck her knife back in her boot after wiping it off on one of the fallen's suit. She closed the clasp and smacked dirt off her leathers. The entire time she was bent over and doing this, the four men in camp just stared like a bunch of teenagers seeing their first supermodel. Cletus and Merle seemed the most affected by it. This probably had to do with their being in an emotionally charged state already.

"So what's the main guy's actual name?" Rachel said as she turned to look at us. She clearly noticed that we were all staring at her because she added, "What?"

"Hmmm?" I said and then coughed. "Uh, nothing. Must just be the elixir. What was your question?"

"The big boss," she said, nodding at Harvey, "what's his name?"

"Frederik," Harvey answered and then guffawed. "Hey wait, you said 'Fred,' right?"

I gave a sideways smile to Rachel. "I sure did."

"I didn't put two and two together because he *hates* being called Fred." He chuckled for a second. "So you know the guy?"

"Not exactly. Lucky guess, I suppose."

We got another communique in from the team at the front lines. It seemed that Fred—or Frederik—had started sending his second wave in. The normals were having a blast, but my crew was starting to run out of steam.

We crested another hill and saw that Fred had set up a basecamp. This was good and bad. It was good because it meant he wasn't going to be moving around; it was bad because there would certainly be sentries around.

Everyone hit the dirt.

"Did you feel anything trigger?" I asked Rachel.

"No, but that doesn't mean we weren't spotted."

Exactly what I was thinking.

I motioned everyone to slowly creep back down until we

were out of visual range from any of the hills on the other side. We could only hope that nobody saw us. With any luck they were all looking in different directions at the time.

But we had to have our bearings, so I crawled back up, recognizing the fact that this suit was completely done for. It was my own fault. I seriously needed to invest in an outfit that was meant for this type of fighting.

Zooming my vision, I caught three sentries. One was directly across from us. He appeared to be sleeping. Another was inline with the campground, nearly right on top of it. The third was in the distance, toward where the rest of my crew and the normals were battling zombies. I guessed that sentry was really there to relay details on the fight.

I couldn't spot any on this side, which seemed odd. Why only cover one visual plane?

"I see only three," I said after getting back with the crew, "and they're all on the other side."

"That don't make sense," Merle said.

"Nope," agreed Cletus.

"Doesn't to me either," I stated, "so keep your eyes open and move carefully."

"He probably just has detectors on this side," noted Rachel. "Or maybe explosives."

That put a dent in my plan. I was hoping to have the two normals skirt around and lay down fire against the zombies once our true purpose in camp became apparent, but they didn't have a connector installed. That meant our fancy glasses wouldn't allow them to spot any bombs. It was one thing to get them to fight along with us, but something else entirely to just blow up while walking along to set up sniper positions.

"You'll have to go with them," I said to Rachel. Her eyebrows went up and she started to speak, but I stopped her. "It's the only way. These guys can't wear the shades."

"I can wear shades," argued Cletus. "Do it all the time."

"Me, too," Merle said with a nod. "Not at night, usually, but I'm quite capable of wearing them."

"These aren't just any shades, gentlemen," I said, and left it at that. "Rachel, it's the only way. You have to keep them safe while Harvey brings me in."

She sighed and nodded.

I knew she didn't like it. Neither did I, but sometimes that's how things rolled out. Besides, it could be for the best anyway since having her throwing magic from afar would be useful in keeping the mages on the ground busy.

"All right, Harvey," I said after checking my weapons to make sure they were set, "you ready to do this?"

"As long as you keep your promise about letting me rip Chip's head off, I'm good."

"You've got my word," I stated with a sharp nod. "Of course, that assumes that you get to him first. If one of these guys shoots him, it's out of my hands."

Harvey frowned, which looked really strange on a bear. "A deal is a deal, Officer Dex."

"It's fine," said Cletus. "We can shoot around him. Right, Merle?"

"It'd help if we knew what he looked like."

"Oh yeah, true." Harvey tapped his cheek while looking up. "He's a little guy about your height," he said, pointing at Cletus. "Wears a black robe and a pointy hat."

"Don't all of the wizards down there do that?" I asked, recalling the quick scan I'd done.

"Yeah, that's true." Harvey snapped his fingers. "Oh yeah, you won't be able to miss him! My wife bought him one of those silly laser signs for his birthday last month. Makes him wear it, too." He leaned in. "She's really pushy. Matriarch of the family and all, you know?"

I frowned. "You're kidding."

"No." He laughed. "The other wizards make fun of him relentlessly because of that sign. Anyway, if you see that, it's Chip."

"What's it say?" I cautiously ventured.

"Chip, the wizard."

CHAPTER 41

$\mathcal{H}$arvey carried me in to camp as if I'd been knocked out. Honestly, it must have looked like he was carrying me across the marital threshold because I was on my back in his massive arms. I was comfortable in my masculinity, but it didn't help to hear Rachel making jokes through the connector.

"Now if you have any questions about your first night together, Ian," she was saying, "make sure to ask them *before* he takes your flower."

"Shut up," I whisper-hissed. "I'm trying to get my head in the game here."

"That's the spirit. Just act like you enjoy it. He'll never know."

I wanted to groan in response, but that would only spur on another comment. Besides, we were getting close to the main players now.

It was show time.

"Where are the rest of them?" asked a snotty sounding man.

"They put up a fight, Chip," Harvey answered evenly. "Me

and this guy were the only two survivors, and he got it worse than I did."

"Unbelievable. You had one job to do, and it wasn't even a difficult job. My sister was right, you are an imbecile."

Okay, so now I understood why Harvey was amped to tear this guy's limbs off. And according to my new werebear pal, Chip's sister was even worse. At least she wasn't here to tag team the poor guy.

"Hey, sis," Chip called out, "your lame excuse for a husband screwed up again."

"What?" a female version of Chip said. I heard the crunching of dirt under feet. "Where are the rest of them, you worthless snake?"

I cracked open an eye and found myself looking at an incredibly attractive woman. She had dark red hair, green eyes, pale skin, and lips so full that they could have been moon bounces. Honestly, it made me grasp how Harvey could manage to put up with her nagging.

"They were killed, along with all our guys."

Harvey's voice had an edge to it. A grit. He was losing his cool. I pinched his arm, hoping to stir the memory that we needed him to keep that facade rolling a little longer. Obviously he caught on because he sighed and grunted.

"Sorry to be obstinate, Matilda," he said like a defeated husband. "I think the speed spell Chip put on me wore me out a bit."

Matilda?

"A real man could handle that spell without a problem," Matilda noted with much disdain. "I'll never understand how you became a werebear at all. Weak-willed, weak-spirited, and weak minded."

To his credit, Harvey didn't reply. I had the feeling that the time of reckoning was nigh, though.

She grunted and said, "Follow me."

Again, I opened an eye and watched her walking in front of us. That body was enough to make me weak in the knees, and in spirit, *and* in mind. Seriously, damn.

Poor Harvey.

"Are we supposed to shoot her?" I whispered up at him.

"Shit," he replied and shook his head.

"Thought not."

I notified Rachel to leave her off the hit list as well. Harvey would take care of them both. Such a shame, I thought as I gave Matilda another gander. Ah well, there are many fish in the sea.

"Supreme Wizard," she announced, dropping to a knee and putting a fist into her opened hand at head height while bowing slightly, "we have brought you mostly what you asked for."

"Why only mostly?" came the response. I couldn't see the face, but that voice fit Shitfaced Fred all right. "There were four, according to my notification runes. Yet I only see one here."

"The others died in battle," she replied meekly.

It was clear that she was afraid of this guy. Considering how she'd just treated Harvey, that was surprising. It either meant Fred was a real bad ass—which he clearly was—or she wasn't as strong-willed, strong-spirited, and strong-minded as she seemed. Could it be that Harvey was just pressing the wrong buttons? I'd seen that kind of thing many times over my years. Well, if we made it out of this alive, I'd have to have a word with him about it. Granted, Matilda would end up doing time for being involved in all of this, but maybe their marriage could be salvaged if he just learned to exert a little control.

"Very disappointing," Fred said as he approached me. "Set him down."

Harvey plopped me on the ground. It didn't feel great, but

I understood why he did it that way. If he'd have gingerly set me down, that would have looked suspicious.

I groaned and began acting like I was waking up.

"What happened?" I said. "Where am I?"

"You've been captured, Mr. Dex," said Fred with a very proud smile.

"Captured where?" I was playing the role a little longer so he wouldn't get suspicious. "Everything is blurry and the sounds are all muffled."

"Well, we can't have that," said Fred and then he flicked his wand at me.

A small bit of energy struck my temple. It didn't hurt. In fact, it made me feel quite clear-headed. Almost too clear, which I assumed happened because I was just faking my concussion symptoms.

"There, that should do it."

"Shitfaced Fred?" I replied, blinking at him in mock surprise. "*You're* the necromancer?"

His eyes grew dark as the wizards around him all sucked in a worried breath. Obviously he didn't like the name I'd selected for him. That made me feel good inside.

"Who told you my nickname?" he asked with a hiss as he leaned in so nobody could hear him. "I haven't been called that in years."

Okay, that was surprising. You've been on this ride with me, so you know I just made up that name from the get-go. I had no insights or intel. There was nothing in the vision that spelled out his name either, let alone his nickname. Maybe this was another skill of mine? Kind of a pointless skill, unless I was destined to be a phone operator in a third-world country at some point in my life.

"Honestly, it was just a guess because of how you looked when I first saw you," I explained almost apologetically. "That, and I like the name Fred."

"Well, it's Frederik, if you please." His irritation remained apparent. He snapped his fingers at Harvey and pointed at me. "Now, we have business to attend to, Mr. Dex, and your assistance is required."

Harvey dragged me to my feet and pushed me to follow behind Fred. With each shove, I noticed that Matilda gave Harvey a hint of admiration. So I *was* right. She was the type of person who wanted a strong hand. I'd seen it on both sides of the fence in relationships. Hell, I preferred the strong hand of Serena, right? Of course I played both ways. Just ask Jasmine. But Matilda's brand of play was different. She liked being *punished*. That's why she was a shit-starter. She would never acquiesce without a fight, but once Harvey earned that respect, she'd be putty in his hands. That, though, all depended on whether or not Harvey was strong enough. I'm not talking physically here, either.

"You realize I'm not going to help you, I hope?" I said to Fred as we approached a table. Beyond the table I spotted Paula seated in one of the chairs. Her eyes were closed. Shit. I swallowed hard but kept my act going. "I don't care how nicely you ask, either."

"I wouldn't dream of *asking* you, Mr. Dex."

"Oh."

If I was being honest, I'd have to say that Fred was kind of terrifying. He was small, sure, and frail, and his face was drawn, and his eyes were sunken into his skull, but there was something even more dark and creepy about him. Beyond the necromancer thing, I mean. He was just…ick.

"What are you planning to do to me?"

His grin was vile. "I'm going to turn you into a zombie, of course."

CHAPTER 42

I drew Boomy so fast that Doc Holiday would have raised an impressed eyebrow. I trained it on Fred. If he wanted to play the kill-Ian-Dex game, it'd take more than simple threats.

Within seconds hands were glowing from the mages on his squad, wizards had their wands up and pointed at me, a set of zombies was closing in, and a couple of werewolves and vampires joined them.

"Put down your weapons and calm yourselves," Fred commanded. He then looked back at me and said, "There you go, Mr. Dex. I'm all yours. You may fire when ready."

I knew taking a shot at him was going to prove pointless, but I needed to stall so that Rachel, Cletus, and Merle could do whatever it was they were planning to do.

"Before I do," I said, "what's been your point of all this?"

"Ah, you wish me to spill the beans of my nefarious plan, eh?"

I shrugged. "Sure, why not?"

"You must watch a lot of movies, Mr. Dex," he said with an old-man's chuckle. "Very well, I shall humor you, though you'll be seeing this unfold firsthand anyway. Of course your perspective will be a bit less clear when that happens."

"Let's not forget who is holding the gun here, Fred."

He sneered. "My name is Frederik. Not Fred. Curb your insolence or I'll make you wish you'd never been born."

I laughed at that. "You just said you're about to kill me, Fred," I said, continuing to push his buttons. "Still not sure where you get that level of confidence seeing as I'm about to put a bullet in you, but delusions seem to be the norm with you crazy bastards." His eye was twitching. "Regardless, if you're going to kill me anyway, what difference does it make about my wishing to have never been born?"

"There are things worse than death, Mr. Dex."

"Who's seen too many movies now, Fred?" I shook my head at him. "Seriously, that was pathetic."

The best part of this entire exchange was seeing all of his minions as they looked from Fred to me to Fred and so on. It was like watching a match at Wimbledon.

"Do you wish to hear of my plans or are you just intent on irritating me to the point of destroying you?"

"Both?" I offered as a possible third option.

"Forget it," he said, looking even more aggravated than before. "I'll just kill you now."

"Wait, wait, wait," I said, shaking the gun at him while wondering where the hell Rachel and crew were. "How about I guess what your dastardly plans are?"

He held up a hand to stop the others from coming in.

"This should prove interesting," he mused. "Fine. Go ahead."

"If it's all the same to you," I added, while lowering Boomy slightly, "I'd rather not have to point this at you the entire time. Gentleman's agreement that I may speak freely and then reset to our current position?" He seemed perplexed by this request, which all played well into my idea.

I needed to put him on edge. "It's just that I think better when I pace back and forth."

"Oh, right," Fred said. "I get that. I'm the same actually."

"Great minds think alike, they say."

"Right." He coughed lightly. "Well, I agree to your terms." He then turned to his crew and said, "Nobody is to take any action against this man until I say so."

They all relaxed.

I stuck Boomy back in his holster and cracked my knuckles. The camp was rather small, but a box of the size that I'd seen in my vision could be hidden anywhere. I had to find it.

"My initial thought," I began as I stepped toward the table, "was that you wanted to systematically terrorize the city until such time that you could just kill off everyone in my department."

I dropped to tie my shoe and glanced under the table. Nothing.

Jumping back up I continued, "But that seemed too easy for someone of your skill. There had to be more going on than was meeting the eye."

The group of chairs where Paula was sat off to the side of the table, with a smaller table sitting in their midst. There was also a mini fridge, which I thought was pretty cool considering Fred was supposed to be a villain and all. Taking care of your people's needs was important, regardless of what you did for a living. On top of the fridge was a framed photograph of Fred in full wizard attire. The word "Master" was etched on the frame at the bottom.

"For a while I had even considered that you were only after me. I was told it was just my ego talking, but you definitely seemed to be going out of your way to coat me with zombie goop."

"I was merely helping you to acclimate to the role you'll soon be playing," he said in a kind way.

"Very generous."

"Think nothing of it."

"But I thought for certain my crew was wrong about my ego." I paused. "Well, they're right about my ego, but I mean specifically the part regarding you coming after me specifically. But then my ego was justified when you kidnapped Paula. You must have known she and I dated for a while."

"I did indeed know, and that's precisely why I took her. I wanted you to come after me."

I nodded and gave her still form another look.

"So there's no soul-sucking or anything going on with her?" I tried to keep hopefulness out of my voice.

"No," he answered. "It was a thought, but I had to use my powers elsewhere. Besides, it's not like she's any threat to me. I *do*, however, plan on making her a zombie as well."

"Well, that's thoughtful."

"Thank you."

The other three chairs were clear and so was the table. But on top of the fridge behind her I spotted a box that looked nearly identical to the one Fred's master had been holding in my vision. Even the etchings looked similar. Not identical, but I'm sure that Fred had made some enhancements over the years. I hadn't spotted it originally because it was sitting behind that picture of Fred.

I spun on my heel, trying to keep my excitement at bay.

"Then it finally hit me," I said while wagging a finger at him as I held a mischievous grin. "You were planning to build an army of zombies through two major channels. The first one was via graves. That was the easiest one."

"Not as easy as you may think," Fred rebutted.

"Necromancy is a challenging art that requires years of dedication. And it ravages your body in the process."

"So I noticed," I said as he showed me his gnarled hands. I opened a channel to Rachel so that she could listen in. "But you wanted to attack in a more prominent way, which brings me to the second channel you decided to use."

"Keep egging him on," Rachel said, "we're closing in."

"The graves brought you enough zombies to kill residents. From there you're planning to raise those you kill, turning them into zombies, and then you'll watch your army grow and grow."

He clapped his hands as I moved back into place and withdrew Boomy, resetting it in position. I had to hand it to Fred that he *had* kept his word about that. Most bad guys wouldn't have.

"Well done, Mr. Dex," he said almost proudly, "though I'd be remiss if I didn't say that my plan wasn't all that complicated to figure out. Why go elegant when you can do the straight and narrow?" It was his turn to pace. "But you did miss one thing, I'm afraid."

"What's that?"

"You, Mr. Dex." He had his hands clasped behind his back. "You're an amalgamite. You have many traits that I can expand once you're under my command." I glanced over at Matilda. Her eyelashes were fluttering. "Killing you is the first step of that because I have no desire to be in a constant battle of wills. But once that's done, you'll be brought back with a mind even more numb than your current one." I felt that I should have been offended by that. "That's when all that you are capable of, Mr. Dex, will be at my disposal."

He stopped and looked at me with questioning eyes.

"We're going to wait for your play," said Rachel, "and then we'll commence."

"Fine," I replied and then glanced up at Fred's cataract-laden eyes. I didn't want him to know I was communicating with Rachel. "Fine, fine, fine. Sensible, too, I must admit."

"Oh," he said, adding a little skip to his step as he returned to his original spot. "I believe I was about here, no?"

"Close enough."

"Please do fire, Mr. Dex," he said with a wink. "I do so wish to get things moving."

"I will, but I have a couple more questions, if you don't mind?"

"Go on."

"What was with the skeletons?" I used the notches on the barrel of Boomy to scratch the side of my head. "I get the zombies, but the skeletons just seemed dumb. I mean, no offense, but what were you thinking there?"

His head was bouncing while I was speaking. Apparently, he agreed with the skeletons being a weak move on his part, but I was still curious as to his reasoning.

"It was another attempt at trying to make the zombies tougher to kill," he explained. "Sadly, I went a little overboard in my planning and ended up with skeletons. They *were* instrumental in my setting triggers against your mages though."

"True, that was cruel indeed."

He waved a dismissive hand. "It's a little late for flattery, Mr. Dex."

"Never hurts to try. You also had a zombie who was speaking to me in full sentences. It was a little creepy, if I were being honest. Were you controlling him directly or something?"

"No," he answered, "but that's a novel idea. I *did* see this vocalization happen with a couple of zombies myself, though. My only guess is that they were freshly dead and therefore able to use their voices better than the others. It was a fortunate happenstance, though, since I've been able to use them for power words."

"So we've noticed."

Fred tapped his watch. "If that's all, Mr. Dex, I would appreciate it if we could get a move on. I have a city to invade, after all."

"You bet, Fred," I said, turning the gun toward the little box.

I fired.

It exploded.

CHAPTER 43

*T*ime seemed to freeze as the light dissipated from the explosion. There was no debris or even a shockwave. It was just a bright light and boom.

"Ha ha!" Fred exclaimed, clapping his hands. "I was right!"

I was baffled.

Shooting the box should have ended everything. Seeing that it didn't meant that this was a trap, especially after Fred's declaration about being right. About what, I had no idea, but it couldn't have been beneficial to me and my team.

"Rachel," I whispered while pretending to check my gun, "don't engage yet. It's a trap."

"I saw that," she answered. "We're going to take a different angle on this. Hang tight."

"Uh…" I said, looking up. "What was it you were right about again?"

"When you bumped into me near Freemont, Mr. Dex, I felt something odd. It was an energy transference of some sort." He looked to be searching for an answer. "I couldn't explain it then, and I'll be honest and say that even now I'm rather confused by precisely what happened, but it felt as though a piece of my history left me."

"Couldn't that just be senility?"

"Cute," he replied with a cheap grin. "Still, something told me that you would know more about me than I'd expected. Thus, when it came time to finally meet you, I took the one thing that held my greatest power, my personal essence, and hid it away." His hands were rubbing together in that evildoer kind of way, which was just a shade over mad scientist style. "Then, as a test, I created another box that was nearly identical. I figured that if you searched for it and destroyed it, my assumption would be correct." He motioned at the spot where the box had been sitting a minute ago. "It seems my supposition was dead on."

What was the point of Flashes if they *told* the bad guy you were getting intel on him?

"Well, I guess that worked out in your favor."

I fired Boomy at him and the bullet stopped an inch in front of his face and dropped.

I sighed.

"Had to try," I said, shrugging.

"It would be foolish of you not to," Fred agreed. "But now that you've put in your pitiful attempt, and noting that I have a lot of firepower standing here that not even you, Mr. Dex, could hope to overcome…. May I suggest that you lay down your weapon and take your medicine?"

"Do it," Rachel said. "I have a plan."

"You sure," I replied, keeping my lips from moving. "I really don't want to be a zombie."

"Do it," she replied more insistently.

I dropped my gun and put my hands up in surrender. Whatever Rachel's plan was, it had better be good. Being dead or undead or reanimated or whatever the hell you wanted to call it sounded pretty dismal, especially since I'd end up in the undignified position of serving this old fart.

"No need to put your hands up, Mr. Dex," he said as two zombies approached me. "If you get rambunctious, we'll deal with you in the roughest of ways, which I'm sure you already know."

"Right."

"Plus, you must also be aware that you'll end up on in my clutches eventually anyway."

"Yep."

"Good, good." He patted the table as a group of wizards began to close in. "Just hop up here and I shall endeavor to make this as painful as possible."

I jumped up on the table and then blinked a few times, wondering if I heard him right.

"Don't you mean you'll make it as *painless* as possible?"

"No, I don't think I did."

A couple of straps launched up from the sides of the table, wrapping around me and tightening to the point where I found it hard to breathe. They were cutting into my flesh, which meant they were ripping my suit. Honestly, I had to invest in more appropriate attire for these adventures.

The wizards began their pygmy-style chanting, causing me to giggle.

"Finding this humorous, Mr. Dex?"

"Love the pygmy stuff," I replied, fighting to keep my wits about me. "It's truly hilarious, Fred."

"It's Frederik!"

"Right, right, sorry. I just thought we were starting to be pals, ya know?"

"Pals?"

"Buds, buddies…friends."

His eyes went wide. "Genuinely?"

"No, Fred. Not at all." I laughed in a mocking way. "You're

about to kill me and turn me into a zombie and you think I'd genuinely want to be friends with you?" Then I cursed myself and tried, "Unless our being pals would make it so you didn't kill me?"

"Enough out of you!" He slapped me with his gnarled hand.

"Damn, Fred," I said with a chuckle as I turned back to him. "You hit like a girl. It's amazing that these people follow you at all. I mean, look at you. Old, frail, hit like a girl…"

A stream of energy flew at me from his fingertips, but bounced off because of the amulet I was wearing.

"For the love of Pete!" he yelled and then reached in and removed the amulet.

Shit.

This time his energy spell worked, and it hurt like hell. My body convulsed as my eyes rolled up into my head. I was hearing someone calmly saying, "Go to the light. Go to the light."

Screw that.

I fought.

I fought hard.

But I was losing. The pain was beyond tolerance and that light was getting bigger and bigger. A scream burst from my mouth that was completely out of my control.

Then everything went black.

CHAPTER 44

I don't know what Rachel's plan was, but I awoke to find the world was very hazy. My head was swimming and I could barely see. Sounds were muffled at best and I was having trouble focusing on anything.

"Get your ass up," Rachel said through the connector.

At least that was coming through loud and clear, and it told me that she was still alive. But I couldn't get the words out to reply. Either I was still magically drugged or I had become a zombie. The way I felt, it made me think it was the later.

"Unn mmmm," was all I could say.

"The restraints are off, Ian," she explained as the sound of popping filled the air near me. Those were Desert Eagles firing. That's one sound I couldn't forget. "Get the hell up and get moving."

My hindbrain kicked into gear and pushed me to move. It took everything in my being to roll over and I instantly regretted it because I'd fallen off the table and was now lying facedown on the ground.

"Ow," I mumbled into the dirt.

"Shit," said Rachel, and then, "Merle, give him some of this."

I felt Merle flipping me onto my back. Then a burning sensation filled my throat as the elixir that Serena had made hit me.

My eyes flew open and I bolted upright.

Two hits of that potion so close together was not fun. Instant headache.

On the plus side, Fred had clearly been unable to complete my transition into zombieism. That was obviously a relief seeing that I had no desire to die. My only thought was that Rachel had gotten there in time to stop whatever ritual that old asshole was performing on me, and my healing capabilities were enough to wrench me from death's grasp.

"What's happening," I said, my vision blurring and correcting in such a way as to make me feel seriously drunk. "This sucks."

"We interrupted his spell and took out three of his mages." She grunted and I felt a stream of heat pass over my head. "I'm starting to run low on reserves, but you needed that hit more than I did."

"Thanks. How is Paula?"

"She's on the ground, we're covering her."

I got up and saw Boomy sitting in the dirt. It took a minute for me to pick it up, but soon I was firing it in the general direction of the bad guys. The bullets did nothing against the magic users, as they were shielded, but the bodyguards were dropping at regular intervals.

"Looks like we've got them on the run," I said between breaths.

"Chief," Chuck yelled through the connector, "I don't know what's going on, but all of the zombies that are still walking just did a one-eighty and are running like hell back your way."

"Joy," I replied, using the table as a stabilizer. "Chase after them please. We're in a difficult spot here."

"On it."

My head was gradually clearing as I kept moving around, getting the elixir through my system. Honestly, I'd rather have been suffering through a massive hangover than dealing with this. If you've ever felt the sensation of your heart flipping over, take that and apply it to your brain.

There was a scream off to my left.

I glanced over to see that Harvey was collecting on his prize. He had Chip up in the air and he was growling for all he was worth. A second later, the crumpled body of his former brother-in-law lay in a heap, pierced by the jagged edge of a rock. It did not look like a fun way to go.

Matilda had obviously seen this, too, because she shrieked angrily and started running at Harvey. But she had to cross by me to get to him. I had just enough energy to knock her on her ass.

Unfortunately, I was still lacking coordination, which meant she landed on her back and I landed on top over her, wedged nicely between her legs. There was nothing sexual about this at all, but when I pushed up I couldn't help but notice her hungry stare. Yep, she needed a firm hand. That firm hand came by way of Harvey the werebear. He clearly did not like the fact that I had mounted his wife. This was apparent because I was in the air and he was looking for another jagged rock.

"Put him down gently," said Cletus, "or I'll stick a hole in ya."

Harvey growled, but set me down.

"Thanks, Cletus."

"Don't mention it."

"Sorry, Harvey," I said. "I was just trying to knock her

over so she couldn't get to you. I'm just a bit clumsy at the moment." To prove that point, I fell over again. "See?"

He picked me back up. "No, it's my bad. I've got a jealous streak."

Matilda stood up and began screaming at him while bullets and magical craziness zoomed all around us. Honestly, this was not the best time for a marital dispute.

"You're about to have the worst night of your life, mister," she was yelling. "And if you think tonight is bad, you just wait until I contact my attorney in the morning. You're going to rue the day you ever…"

Harvey had clearly had enough. His eyes were glowing yellow. This wasn't going to end well.

He turned to her, picked her up to face level, and let out such a ferocious roar that everyone literally stopped firing bullets and magic. It was *that* intense.

Matilda said, "Ooooooh," and then passed out.

"Get down," Rachel yelled as a bolt of energy flew over my head a second later.

Harvey was hovering over his wife, protecting her from the onslaught. Obviously he still loved her, which I could understand from a physical point of view—though I suppose that's technically lust—but I didn't get the personality mix. Still, he had to have seen what had just happened, but he may not have connected the dots.

"Harvey, I gotta tell you something," I said, thinking that if we *did* make it out of this alive, he may just be able to patch up his marriage. Again, Matilda was going to end up doing time for her involvement in this little bit of fun, but at least she'd have something to look forward to when she got out. "Matilda has a thing for powerful men. It's probably why she married you. I don't mean abusive here, though I have little doubt that she'd thoroughly enjoy a good spanking, I'm talking about someone who is very strong and controlling. You know, like a werebear, for example."

"What?" he said, glaring at me. "Her? But she's such a dominant bitch."

"That's because she's not the kind who willingly submits," I explained. "She needs to be pushed. Trust me, I've got *a lot* of experience with this sort of thing."

Matilda came to and said, "What happened?"

"You're a bitch, that's what," Harvey said, "and I'm sick and tired of it. If you want to get an attorney tomorrow, go for it; otherwise, you'd best get your shit together and start treating me the way I deserve to be treated."

"Oh, Harvey," Matilda said with a mesmerized glow in her eyes.

He turned to me with a shocked look.

I shrugged. "Told ya."

CHAPTER 45

*W*e weren't out of this mess yet.

Zombies were zooming in behind us and they were only about thirty seconds out. Many of them were turning to dust since the rest of my crew was firing like mad at them from behind. There was no way they'd get them all, though.

"We need to find that damn box," I yelled right before a fireball caught my shoulder and spun me through the air to crash into the table I'd been dying on earlier. I pushed myself back up. "Okay, that hurt. I don't suppose anyone has seen my amulet?"

"It's on the ground over by Fred," yelled Harvey.

"My name is Frederik," screamed the old necromancer as he launched an energy blast at Harvey.

But it was blocked.

By Matilda.

"Nobody shoots at my man," she said with a sinister stare.

Then she launched a volley back at Fred. It wasn't powerful enough for the necromancer to be fazed by it, but it was enough to stop me from worrying about whose side she

213

was on. Probably her own. As long as Harvey wore the pants, though, she'd go along with whatever he wanted.

Ah, love. Strange, quirky, and full of surprises.

"Looks like Matilda's joined our side," I said through the connector. "That'll look good on her record, if she makes it to trial."

"Don't care," Rachel replied. "Trying to get Cletus and Merle through for a shot at that damn magical box."

"Where is it?"

She pointed.

I followed the direction of her finger and used zoom to pinpoint the box. It was being held by a stern-looking vampire who stood within feet of Fred. This one had runes that perfectly matched the one from my vision, and there was a glow connecting it to Fred.

"Take care of Paula," I commanded with a look at Rachel.

"I got her."

"Thanks." I grabbed Harvey by the arm and pointed. "Do you think you can throw me over there?"

He grabbed me without answering and I found myself sailing through the air. I wasn't ready for that, to be honest. I'd been on more of a fact-finding mission when I'd asked the question, but his distance was perfect. I crashed right into the vampire, knocking the box from his hands while simultaneously having the wind knocked out of me.

But who needs to breathe?

I snatched up the box and stuck Boomy on it.

Fred's face went completely white.

"No," he said frantically. "Stop! Everyone stop!"

They did. Including the zombies that were closing in from behind us. Again, the world silenced.

"You can't destroy that," he said, licking his lips. "If you do, I'll die. Everything I've created will die."

"Technically, they're already dead, right?"

"Huh?" He looked unsure for a moment. "Yes, yes, they are, but I mean they'll no longer be animated."

"I don't see a problem with that, personally," I said matter-of-factly.

"Please, no, I'm begging you." He actually got down on his knees, which was kind of creepy. "It was nearly one hundred years of work."

"That's a shame, Fred," I said sadly. "Honestly, a man of your power could have done some decent stuff with all that time instead of creating a box of doom. What is it with you evil overlords? If you just channeled your abilities into something good, the world would be such a better place."

"Thanks, Oprah," he replied and then paled some more. "Sorry, sorry. You're right, of course. I've been a bad man. A very very bad man. I'll change. I promise. Just don't destroy that box."

I knew that the Directors wanted to get their hands on this guy, and I couldn't rightly blame them. Fred was powerful. He'd probably be able to dump enough intel to help the magic community build blockers against all this necromancy crap. Honestly, I just wanted to end this guy. In my estimation, he was *too* strong. If they put him in prison, he'd slowly work his way out and then be on the rampage again. He was too set in his ways.

But my job was to bring him in, if possible.

"All right, Fred," I said, pulling the gun away from the box, "if you'll play nice, let us put the cuffs on you, and all that, we'll take you in. The Directors want to speak with you anyway."

"Yes, yes," he replied with much enthusiasm, never taking his eyes off the box. "Whatever you say."

He was obsessed. I moved his rune-covered prize slowly around. He followed it like a dog would a treat. That was strange, but it's not what had me worried.

Three things set me on edge. The first was that Fred's eyes were somehow getting darker and glowing at the same time; the second thing was that the box was starting to grow warm in my hands and there was a tingling sensation running up my arm; and the third thing was noting that there was a pygmy-sounding chant being done as a whisper from Fred's unmoving mouth.

"Ian!" yelled Rachel as the box lit up.

A light poured from it directly at Fred's open mouth. His entire body was being engulfed by it. It was as though he'd swallowed the sun.

In one fluid motion, I launched the box straight up into the air, trained Boomy on it, and fired.

CHAPTER 46

*I*t was pretty amazing how powerful that explosion was, but the weirdest part is *how* it blew up.

Nobody but Fred was impacted.

I guess that had to do with the connection he'd built between himself and that box. This explained why he didn't die during that explosion I saw in the vision. The box killed *his* master, but left everyone else intact.

Obviously it was his last shot at salvaging his nefarious plans, but all it ended up doing was localizing the destruction. Good thing, too, or we'd have all died from it. If what happened to Fred was any indication of what would have happened to us, I can honestly say that it did not look enjoyable. He was obliterated. There were bits of him all over the place. If even one decent-sized chunk of his flesh could be found, I'd be impressed. You could find tons of his blood and such everywhere, though. In fact, we were all wiping ourselves down because of it.

My poor suit.

All of the zombies dropped to the ground with a collective thud. The apprentice wizards were blinking and looking around as if in shock. The same was happening with the bodyguards.

"What's going on?" I said to Harvey. "How come they all look confused, but you don't?"

"Your guess is as good as mine," he replied with his hands up. Then he said, "Wait." He turned to Matilda. "Why is everyone looking confused?"

She was staring at him with judging eyes. It was clear to me that she was definitely in need of a short leash and while I didn't know Harvey all that well, he just didn't seem the type to hold it.

"It was his spell," she answered. "He had all of them under it."

"Why not you?"

"Because I'm a higher level, Harvey," she replied with a sneer.

"Watch yourself, woman," Harvey stated with a growl.

Matilda cooed in response, seemingly melting from Harvey's demeanor. Like I said, I know how to call them. Honestly, I'd first thought that Harvey was into that kind of thing seeing how their roles were originally reversed, but it was clear that side of the fence did nothing for him besides cause irritation and loneliness. Again, though, he just seemed to be a really nice guy, so I had the feeling that he'd never last as the dominant type, especially since Matilda was going to constantly make him work for it.

Time to wash my hands of this problem.

The rest of my crew came up the hill, looking haggard. I completely understood that. We all were going to need a little rest and relaxation at this point, especially those of us who drank that elixir. Cletus and Merle would be wiped out for a week. I'd have to see if I could get them a room comped or something.

"You okay?" said Rachel, eyeing me carefully.

"Yeah, why?"

"That box had a trigger on it," she replied, not getting too close. "I saw something jump from it right when you shot it. Oh…" She pointed at the ground near my feet. The amulet was laying just a few steps away from me. She reached down and picked it up by its string and peered inside. Her eyes widened. "You're one lucky bastard, Ian."

"What is it?"

"Eradication spell, from the looks of it."

"Oh, that's sounds nice."

"It's not."

"Obviously." I chewed my lip wondering if I really wanted to know what an eradication spell did, aside from eradicate something, of course. I gave in to my curiosity. "What would it have done?"

"Eradicate you."

I groaned. "I know that, Rachel, but how?"

"Oh, it would've split you into dust like the nanites did to the zombies."

I gulped and looked around.

There were a mass of worried faces, and they all belonged to Fred's minions. Honestly, they looked horrified.

I turned to Matilda and asked, "Do they know what they've done?"

She nodded.

"Did they have any control over it?"

"No."

Good. That meant that most of these people were going to be let off without punishment. Matilda wouldn't be one of them, of course. She'd already admitted that her wrongdoing was by choice. Chances were she'd get a couple of years in high-security and then would have to wear a magic-canceling anklet for a while.

"Harvey?" said Portman as he approached. "What the hell are you doing here?"

They went off into a conversation about things while Rachel and I explained the details of what had occurred to Griff, Chuck, Jasmine, and Felicia. Felicia was in full werewolf mode herself, which didn't happen often. She always seemed self-conscious about it when it happened. I didn't say a word.

"Serena," I called through the connector, "we're all clear here. The necro is dead."

"And the zombies?"

"Dead...again."

"Excellent. I'll work with Portman's folks and tell everyone that the show is over. We'll take care of the logistics."

"Thanks."

"Anyone need healing?"

"I think we're good," I replied. "We'll be back soon."

Paula was in a daze when I approached her.

"How are you feeling?" I asked.

"Not great," she replied, sounding like she was rather drunk. "That bastard kidnapped me, you know?"

"I do, yes. But he's dead now and you'll be fine."

"Dead?" She gave me a glare. "You promised me an exclusive with him, Ian."

"Out of my hands, I'm afraid."

"Isn't it always?"

"Would you have rather I'd have let him kill you?" Her eyes shot open as she wobbled slightly in the chair. "That's right, Paula, he was planning to make you a zombie."

"That would have been bad."

Her eyes were drooping, so I pushed her back gently in the chair and kissed her on the forehead.

She fell asleep.

I walked over to Cletus and Merle. These two had turned out to be dynamos. I honestly couldn't believe how well they stood up to this level of chaos.

"I have to say, guys, you two were pretty incredible."

"Aw shucks," replied Cletus with a wave of his hand.

Merle shrugged. "Just havin' fun is all."

"Honestly, your skill with those guns was damn well on par with ours."

They looked at each other for a second and then started laughing. Obviously there was an inside joke going on. Or maybe I'd said something that could have been construed as toilet humor? I replayed my last sentence and couldn't spot anything wrong.

"We gotta tell ya something, buddy," Merle said. "We ain't a couple of guys with advanced degrees and such."

"You're not?"

"Nah," Cletus piped up, "we both work at the Little Rock Paranormal Police Department."

"What?" I said, giving them both a more careful study. "But you're normals, right?"

"I'm an incubus, actually," Merle replied with a wink.

"You?" He wasn't even close to standard incubus material. "Seriously?"

"Don't be judging this book by its cover, now. I got some moves that'll keep the ladies purrin' for weeks."

"Ew," I said, not wanting to know that. "What about you, Cletus?"

"I'm an incubus, too."

That hat. That t-shirt. That painted-on squint. "No fucking way."

"Yep. That's why we come to Vegas on vacation a couple times a year. You'd be amazed how much of that 'What happens in Vegas, stays in Vegas' stuff is due to us."

JOHN P. LOGSDON & CHRISTOPHER P. YOUNG

"True that," said Merle with a laugh. "I gotta say them zombies is a new one on us. That was fun."

"What about the lottery?" I asked, feeling somewhat perplexed by all of this.

"That bit was true, actually," answered Cletus with a big grin. "Gonna stick with the force, though. It's just too much fun not to."

Rachel stepped into our midst and looked them both over for a few moments.

"Each of you is an incubus?"

"Yes, ma'am," replied Merle.

"We sure is," agreed Cletus.

She walked around, slowly sizing them up. Then she began nodding.

"What are you doing?" I asked.

She gave me an evil grin, put her arms around the shoulders of the Little Rock PPD boys, and said, "Planning my next two days."

CHAPTER 47

The good news was that the impending zombie apocalypse was squashed by my very capable team. The bad news was that I had to go and meet with the Directors about it.

"We were pleased to know that Ms. Rose was retrieved successfully," said O, "though it's a shame you couldn't have brought the necromancer in. Interrogating him would have proved beneficial."

"Agreed, O," said Silver.

That was odd. They only tended to agree with each other after some verbal jousting first. Maybe they'd had a conversation to clear the air? I kind of hoped that *wasn't* the case. I'd rather they be at each other's throats than at mine.

"I gave him the opportunity," I explained, "but he wouldn't have anything to do with it."

Unfortunately, I didn't have any of Fred's remnants to prove my argument because I'd taken a shower *before* my meeting this time.

"And you said that the rest of those involved were under some type of controlling spell?" asked Zack.

223

"Yes, sir. Well, most of them anyway. There were two who weren't. One is dead and the other is in custody."

"We should put everyone else through post-traumatic care," O noted. "Being under the control of an evil wizard is quite horrific."

"I would imagine that to be true, O," said Silver.

I furrowed my brow at this, being that it was the second time they agreed without fuss.

"I would also think the one they brought into custody would do well to have counseling, no?"

"Agreed, Silver," O replied. "I think that's an excellent suggestion."

"Are you douchebags dating now or something?" EQK piped up. "Or maybe you've gone to couples counseling? By the Great Pixie, it's starting to make me sick."

I had to cover my mouth at that one. Leave it to EQK to say what I was thinking, most of the time anyway. Sometimes he went overboard, which was saying something coming from me. This time, though, he was dead on.

"We'll always have our differences, EQK," O said, "but we're a team and so we had a discussion to work things out."

"Did this discussion include wine, moonlight, and a Barry White album playing in the background by chance?" Then EQK grunted and said, "Blech! I'm gonna puke."

"All right, EQK," Zack said sternly, "that's enough. You're the cause of the majority of the problems in this group, and you know it."

"Yeah, so? What's your point?"

"My point is that these two are trying to make things better for everyone and you don't like that."

"Again, not understanding where you're going with this," EQK replied after a few seconds. "Maybe you're just having fun stating the obvious?"

Zack growled. "I'm saying that it would serve you well to learn how to be more diplomatic like they have."

"Oh, I see," EQK said. "Do you really think so?"

"I do."

"Huh. I'll have to think about that."

Why did I have the feeling that an outburst was coming? I'd been reporting to these guys for way too long and there was no way that little pixie was going to play nice. At least not *that* quickly. But the others were gullible. Well, O and Zack anyway. Silver was likely thinking the same way I was. Of course, he may also have been wearing rose-colored glasses at the moment considering how he and O were getting along.

"Maybe we could work together," Zack suggested. "Like O and Silver did."

"Would you really do that?"

"Of course. We're a team, EQK."

"Hmmm. I'll tell you what, Zack." Here it comes. "I'll go ahead and do this little meeting with you as soon as you've found your balls. How's that sound?"

"My balls?" Zack sounded genuinely confused.

"Yeah, those tiny orbs you used to have dangling between your legs, you girl."

"Hey now," said O in a dire voice, "let's not have any of that in chambers!"

"Oh, go play with your wand," EQK shot back.

Silver laughed out loud at that. I could tell it was an unintentional laugh due to the snort that preceded it, but that only made it more pronounced.

"What the hell are you laughing at, Silver?" O demanded.

And that's when they started up their bickering again. Everyone but EQK, anyway. While I couldn't see him, I had the distinct feeling that he was sitting with his arms crossed and a triumphant look on his face.

CHAPTER 48

The Three Angry Wives pub was a welcoming reprieve from the events of the last few days. Drowning my memories in glasses of bourbon wouldn't take it all away, but it'd at least provide a bit of a vacation. What I needed was sleep, and I'd get it…later.

Right now I was dealing with the fact that Rachel was currently rolling in the hay with a couple of incubuses. I frowned. Maybe the term was "incubi?" Either way, I didn't like it. I don't think I was jealous…or maybe I was? Shit, I don't know. I just didn't like it.

I groaned and drained the contents of my glass.

"Glad to see you again," said the voice of a familiar man. It was Gabe. "Mind if I join you?"

"It's a free country," I replied, motioning for him to sit.

He took the seat on the other side of the table. Tonight he had on a charcoal gray suit with a black shirt and gray tie. The guy knew how to dress.

"Nice suit."

"Thank you."

"Your Flashes thing worked," I said while signaling the waiter to bring me another glass full. "Sort of."

Gabe didn't say anything. He merely looked at me questioningly.

"First off, I didn't even know it *was* a thing until I bumped into Shitfaced Fred and it launched itself. Made me wobbly as hell."

"Yes, that's how these things work, I'm afraid," he said almost apologetically. "They reveal themselves as needed and you learn to control them."

I found it interesting that he didn't flinch at or question the name I'd given the necromancer. Did he know the guy? If so, he'd have to have known him well enough to be familiar with the nickname.

"Did you know Fred?"

He nodded. "When we were younger."

I studied Gabe again. He had the look of a man in the middle years. Fit, yes, but mature. That didn't mean anything, though. Griff and Serena were both hundreds of years old, but nobody who didn't know their personnel files would have any clue about that.

Obviously Gabe wasn't going to provide any more details.

I grunted. "Anyway, you said last time that you were around to help me or something like that."

"Yes."

"Aside from dumping magic words on me that cause weirdness to happen while making me fuzzy and unbalanced," I said holding up my glass, "what can you do for me?"

"There is a path that must be followed, Mr. Dex," he answered, "and I'm going to lead you down it."

"Can't we just skip to the end of the path?" I asked as the effects of the alcohol began taking hold. "I'm a pretty resilient guy, you know?"

"Unfortunately, no. Dumping everything on you at once would kill you, regardless of how tough you are." His eyes met mine. "You're needed here, Mr. Dex. There are more of these ubernaturals coming and you must stand against them. Nobody else can."

I didn't know if that last bit was true. My team had done a pretty bang up job of fighting these last two sets. Yeah, I had special skills that helped our cause, and I suppose it was fair to say that the vision crap Gabe laid on me *did* make it so we could knock out Fred in the end. But couldn't the little Flashes thing be installed in anyone?

"How do you know about all this, Gabe?"

He smiled and looked away. "I can't tell you that."

"Why not?"

"*Time* will reveal all things, Mr. Dex," he said, looking at his watch. "And *time* is one thing we don't have much of."

He stood up and grabbed his coat as the word "time" echoed through my skull. Damn it, he was doing it again.

"You just sat down," I said in confusion, "and you're already leaving?"

"Again, Mr. Dex," he replied, "*time* is not on our side. There is much to do."

"What the hell do you keep emphasizing that word for?" I called out as he walked toward the exit. "I know it's going to screw with me somehow, but how?"

The door shut behind him.

I sighed as the TV caught my eye.

It was Paula Rose, but she wasn't the one doing the interviewing. Someone else was asking her questions. That meant she was acting on behalf of The Spin and not the news on SN-50. I guess that made sense seeing that I was sitting in a restaurant intended for normals. Obviously the booze was working its magic.

"...and it was a great success," Paula was saying. "So much

so that Post Apocalyptic Unlimited will be officially opening its doors in thirty days. Customers will be able to spend a fun-filled night using paintball guns to hunt 'zombies' and everything. I've been asked to be a member on the board of directors as well."

I gave a quick chuckle into my drink while shaking my head.

"Good for you, Paula." I drained the glass. "Good for you."

Thanks for Reading

If you enjoyed this book, would you please leave a review at the site you purchased it from? It doesn't have to be a book report… just a line or two would be fantastic and it would really help us out!

John P. Logsdon
www.JohnPLogsdon.com

John was raised in the MD/VA/DC area. Growing up, John had a steady interest in writing stories, playing music, and tinkering with computers. He spent over 20 years working in the video games industry where he acted as designer and producer on many online games. He's written science fiction, fantasy, humor, and even books on game development. While he enjoys writing lighthearted adventures and wacky comedies most, he can't seem to turn down writing darker fiction. John lives with his wife, son, and Chihuahua.

Christopher P. Young

Chris grew up in the Maryland suburbs. He spent the majority of his childhood reading and writing science fiction and learning the craft of storytelling. He worked as a designer and producer in the video games industry for a number of years as well as working in technology and admin services. He enjoys writing both serious and comedic science fiction and fantasy. Chris lives with his wife and an ever-growing population of critters.

CRIMSON MYTH PRESS

Crimson Myth Press offers more books by this author as well as books from a few other hand-picked authors. From science fiction & fantasy to adventure & mystery, we bring the best stories for adults and kids alike.

www.CrimsonMyth.com

Made in the
USA
Middletown, DE